Ana

Heart-breaker and heart-mender.
Mess-maker and trouble-maker.
Throws things into the sky.
Disobedient even in death.

Jessica

Tries and fails to keep herself
together. Addicted to suffering.
Wishes she could sleep under
church pews. Bites people.

Iridian

Sees so much detail of the world,
but cannot see herself. Wants her
life to consist of paper and ink.
Apologizes too much.

Rosa

Gifted with a better heart than
most. Destined to ease the
sufferings of God's smallest
creatures. Not afraid of the dark
or of getting blood on her hands.

"A MAGICAL LITTLE WOMEN FOR OUR TIMES."
—JULIA ALVAREZ, author of *How the García Girls Lost Their Accents*

PRAISE FOR *TIGERS, NOT DAUGHTERS*

"Move over, Louisa May Alcott! Samantha Mabry has written her very own magical *Little Women* for our times."
        —Julia Alvarez, author of *How the García Girls Lost Their Accents*

"Samantha Mabry is just a beautiful writer . . . You should definitely read it."
        —Veronica Roth, *New York Times* bestselling author of the Divergent series

"Ferocious and gorgeously crafted. I loved it."
        —Courtney Summers, *New York Times* bestselling author of *Sadie*

"No one writes the line between Real and Not Real like Samantha Mabry, and no one had better mess with the Torres sister-tigers, either."
        —E. K. Johnston, *New York Times* bestselling author of *Star Wars: Ahsoka*

"This book is its own piece of art—albeit one that feels in conversation with its inspirations. Mabry's language and tone are both lush and poetic, but that doesn't stop these tiger girls from having teeth."
        —NPR

"A shivery, magical exploration of the power of sisterhood."   —*People*

"The National Book Award–nominated author spins another hauntingly moving tale of teenhood with this story of sisters mourning one of their own, only to realize she might still be walking among them . . . somehow."
        —*Entertainment Weekly*

"Samantha Mabry gives us paranormal magical realism at its best with her latest YA novel."
        —*Ms.* magazine

"One of the most crucial voices in young adult literature." —*Bustle*

★ "Mabry speaks gracefully to the transformative power of grief and the often messy (even violent) road to letting go."
—*Publishers Weekly*, starred review

★ "Mabry's third novel has echoes of *The Virgin Suicides* . . . The evocative language and deft characterization will haunt—and empower—readers." —*Kirkus Reviews*, starred review

★ "A lyrical contemporary YA with a dose of magical realism [and] an empowering portrait of grief, sisterhood and resilience."
—*Shelf Awareness*, starred review

★ "*Little Women* meets *The Virgin Suicides* with a magical realist twist in this evocative and lovely novel." —*SLJ*, starred review

★ "Borrowing elements of magical realism and Latinx folklore, this is a story that is often uncomfortable; in its quest to explore grief, family, and the traumas inflicted by each, it lays its characters utterly and unforgettably bare." —*Booklist*, starred review

★ "An appealingly unsettling infusion of ambiguous faith and unexplained miracles." —*BCCB*, starred review

"The kind of story that digs its claws deep into you . . . [It] will haunt your thoughts long after you've finished reading." —*The Nerd Daily*

"This fierce, unforgettable whirlwind of a novel, a wondrous mix of ghost story and drama of sisterly rebellion, holds the reader in thrall from the first sentence to the final page." —*The Buffalo News*

"Atmospheric and evocative . . . This book is as if you took *The Virgin Suicides*, mixed it with *Little Women* and weaved it all together with *King Lear*. Read it, if you are a fan of any of these titles." —*The Young Folks*

Tigers, Not Daughters

Tigers, Not Daughters

SAMANTHA MABRY

ALGONQUIN 2021

Published by
Algonquin Young Readers
an imprint of Algonquin Books of Chapel Hill
Post Office Box 2225
Chapel Hill, North Carolina 27515-2225

a division of
Workman Publishing
225 Varick Street
New York, New York 10014

LIBRARY OF CONGRESS CATALOGING-IN-PUBLICATION DATA
Names: Mabry, Samantha, author.
Title: Tigers, not daughters / Samantha Mabry.
Description: Chapel Hill, North Carolina : Algonquin Books of Chapel Hill, 2020. |
    Audience: Ages 14 and up. | Audience: Grades 10–12. | Summary: "Three sisters
    in San Antonio are shadowed by guilt and grief over the loss of their oldest sister,
    who still haunts their house"—Provided by publisher.
Identifiers: LCCN 2019037812 | ISBN 9781616208967 (hardcover) | ISBN
    9781643750545 (ebook)
Subjects: CYAC: Sisters—Fiction. | Family problems—Fiction. | Grief—Fiction. |
    Ghosts—Fiction. | Hispanic Americans—Fiction.
Classification: LCC PZ7.1.M244 Tig 2020 | DDC [Fic]—dc23
LC record available at https://lccn.loc.gov/2019037812

ISBN 978-1-64375-131-3 (PB)

10 9 8 7 6 5 4 3 2 1
First Paperback Edition

For my students

The Night the Torres Sisters Tried to Run Away from Southtown

THE WINDOW TO Ana Torres's second-story bedroom faced Hector's house, and every night she'd undress with the curtains wide open, in full view of the street. We'd witnessed this scene dozens—*hundreds*—of times, but still, each night Ana had us perched there, pained and floating on the edge of something tremendous.

With her back to us, Ana would strip off her shirt and her bra—that bra made of white cotton, the fabric so thin we could see the shimmer of her sandstone skin through it—and toss them onto the floor at the foot of her never-made bed. She'd lift up her arms, stretch her spine like a cat, and roll her head side to side to ease out the kinks in her neck. She'd run her fingers through her long, ink-black hair before gracefully winding it up into a knot. Then she'd turn—so slowly it made our eyes gloss with tears. She'd sigh and gaze through her window—never straight at our faces, which were always twisted tightly with hope—but always past us, over the top of the crooked oak tree in her front yard, over the top of Hector's two-story house, over the tops of tilted palms several streets away, to some far-away place. She'd have this wistful expression on her face, like she was waiting for something, or some*one,* to come down from the night sky and take her away.

We were barely fifteen, and Ana was nearly eighteen, but we were convinced that we could be her heroes. We could be the ones to rescue her and take her wherever she wanted to go. Up and over into New Mexico? No problem. Down into Matamoros? Just say when. Peter knew the basics when it came to driving a car, and Luis had close to fifty bucks stashed away in a drawer. We would do what-ever it took and would suffer any number of indignities to be with her, this girl of our young, fresh dreams, to save her from our old neighborhood, with its old San Antonio families and its traditions so strong and deep we could practically feel them tugging at our heels when we walked across our yards. We wouldn't have cared if Ana made fun of our gangly bodies, our terrible, squeaky voices, the way no deodorant could come close to covering up our puberty-stink, or the very, very dumb things we inevitably would say.

Just tell us where you want to go, Ana. And we'll take you there.

We never got the chance.

Just over a year ago, on an unusually warm spring night during Fiesta, Ana Torres opened her second-story window and stuck out her head. She was checking to make sure the street was clear before she latched on to the sturdy branches of the old oak tree. She shimmied down the wide trunk, and once the soles of her flip-flops landed on the patchy grass, she dusted off the bits of bark from her palms and turned her gaze up.

There, at Ana's window, was her sixteen-year-old sister, Jessica. Jessica tossed down a pink backpack, then a blue one, then two matching tweed suitcases like the kind traveling salesmen used to carry back when there were such people as traveling salesmen. Ana caught each of them, one after the other, her knees buckling only slightly under the weight. She set them in a row near the base of the tree and looked up again, to watch Jessica hitch her left leg awkwardly through the window and then reach for the nearest branch with unsure hands.

Even from across the street at Hector's house, we could see Jessica's lips pulled back and her teeth clamped together in cold determination. She was gripping too hard—first to the window frame, then to the branches. It was obvious

3

she'd never done anything like this before. Her fingers were popping the leaves loose, and the soles of her high-tops were chipping off bits of bark. Both the leaves and the bark were fluttering to the ground, right to where Ana was bouncing on the balls of her feet. We could tell Ana wanted to call out to her sister. She couldn't say anything, though—couldn't risk it—because the base of the tree, right by the row of luggage, was directly in front of their dad's bedroom window.

By now, fifteen-year-old Iridian—the girls, we realized, were making their escape in birth order—was leaning half-way out the window, scowling at Jessica's slow and clumsy progress. She kept glancing nervously over her shoul-der, then down to the top of her sister's head. Her fingers drummed against the window frame. Finally, she couldn't wait anymore. She pulled her hair back into a quick bun and climbed out. Her movements—like Ana's—were solid and sure. She knew exactly where to grip, how to shift her balance, when to inhale, when to exhale. Soon though, Iridian was forced to pause and dangle, waiting for Jessica. She glanced to the window above, where the youngest of the Torres sisters, Rosa, who was twelve, was starting to emerge.

Finally, Jessica hit the ground—hard and flat-footed. Her arms pinwheeled like a cartoon character's until she caught her balance. Seconds later, Iridian swung off a high branch and landed in a crouch in the grass. She pulled her hair out from her bun, and the strands spilled across her shoulders.

Now that the three of them—Ana, Jessica, and Iridian—were all on solid ground, they looked up in unison. Rosa was wearing a calf-length dress because Rosa always wore a calf-length dress. Tonight, though, in honor of Fiesta, the front of that dress was covered in medals—like awards, like pins in the style of a Purple Heart, except most of hers were made of plastic with bright, multicolored ribbons attached to them. As Rosa was suspended with just the tip of one bulky shoe braced against the window frame, the fabric of her dress caught in a breeze, and we wouldn't have been surprised if, instead of climbing down to join her sisters, Rosa climbed *up* into the tallest, most tender branches of the tree to search for birds' nests or pluck off the prettiest leaf or just be closer to the stars in the night sky. We'd always thought that if Rosa were an element, she'd be air, the lazy kind that gets tossed around a room when a ceiling fan is on its lowest setting.

Rosa did decide to climb down instead of up, but just as she was about to take the final, short leap to the ground, her dress got caught on something—maybe the sharp nub of a snapped-off limb—and her skirt was hoisted up to her ribs, exposing not just her pale underwear but the bottom edge of her bra. Our breaths caught—all at the same time. We saw Ana reach over and grip Jessica's wrist. Iridian took a step forward, then stopped, then put her hand over her mouth. Rosa shifted her weight, released one hand from the tree branch and pulled—once, twice—before the fabric gave way. Then, finally, she leapt.

From there, the girls didn't hesitate. They each grabbed a piece of luggage and were gone, down Devine Street and then north and away from Southtown.

For a moment, we just stood there, shoulder to shoulder at Hector's bedroom window, our skin buzzing with the kind of feeling a person gets before jumping off a high cliff into water: bravery mixed with low-level terror. Eventually, we looked at one another. We knew that *this* was our moment. We crept out of Hector's room and tiptoed down the stairs. One by one, we pushed through the Garcias' squeaky storm door and stepped out into the night.

If the Torres sisters were headed north and carrying luggage, we figured their destination was the Greyhound station on St. Mary's and Martin, even though it was over a mile away and on the other side of downtown. Sure enough, when we got to the end of Devine, we saw the sisters hustling in that direction. We didn't know for sure where they'd catch a bus to, but if we had to guess, we would've said the girls were heading south, to the Rio Grande Valley, where their aunt Francine lived in a big house in the middle of the orange groves.

Ana led the way. Behind her was Iridian. Then Rosa. Bringing up the rear was Jessica. Her suitcase was so heavy it banged against the side of her leg with every step, and she had to keep switching it from her right hand to her left and back.

All warm, star-flecked spring nights in downtown San Antonio bring out the tourists, but this night was different from the other warm, star-flecked nights. The girls were making their getaway on one of the busiest nights of the year, during Fiesta, when the streets were packed, even in the middle of the night—and not just packed with tourists, but with locals draped in medal-covered sashes and wearing crowns made from paper flowers. They were out in droves to celebrate the Texians who fought long ago in the battles of the Alamo and San Jacinto. And even when we were still a couple of blocks away from downtown proper, we could hear the music—the blare of horns, the percussive thumps of guitars. Little bits of colored crepe paper floated through air and covered the sidewalks and the streets.

The girls chose to run away during Fiesta probably because they thought they could disappear in the huge, ambling crowd and no one would notice them, and maybe that was a good plan. We, however, could do nothing *but* notice them. None of the Torres sisters was particularly tall—Iridian was the tall*est*, but still not tall. Their heads didn't bob above the crowd, but we could still see it shift and part as the girls pushed through. We followed, shouldering and ducking our way through people who smelled like beer and cinnamon and drugstore cologne. We thought we could stay hidden and that *we* could go unnoticed, but once the sisters had finally plowed through the crowd's northernmost edge and were picking up their pace, Jessica, who was still bringing up the rear, glanced over her shoulder and saw us.

She stopped. Her eyes narrowed. We froze. She advanced.

"Shit," Jimmy squeaked.

Even with a little square of pink crepe paper stuck just above her right eyebrow, Jessica Torres was still scary as hell. It seemed like she was always, *always* angry. In kindergarten, she bit a teacher on the wrist because snack time was over and he tried to take away her peanut butter crackers. In junior high, she keyed Jenny Sanchez's mom's car because she didn't like the color of it, and just this last December, she got detention for three days after she'd jammed the tip of a lead pencil into Muriel Contreras's pinky finger. The lead is still in there. Muriel tries to say it's a freckle, but everyone knows the truth.

For a moment, there on the far edge of the Fiesta celebration, none of us spoke. Jessica stared us down. Her teeth were clamped together, bared slightly, just like they were when she was climbing down that tree. The other Torres sisters—realizing Jessica was no longer with them—halted and spun around.

It was Hector who finally mustered up some courage. He cleared his throat and asked, "Where are you going?"

"We can help," Calvin quickly chimed in.

Ana took a step forward. She shrugged off her heavy backpack and slid herself in front of Jessica. She looked us over, met each of us in the eye for the briefest moment, but said nothing. A breeze caught her hair, lifting the strands, blowing them in our direction.

We'd never been this close to Ana Torres before, and it was disorienting. She was so, so beautiful. We'd imagined before—*many* times—what she might've smelled like. Maybe it was roses, vanilla, lemons, or maybe the first, fresh slice of white bread pulled from the plastic sleeve. But until then, we never truly knew.

It was laundry. She smelled like laundry, like dryer sheets mixed with a little stubborn sweat.

"We can help," Calvin repeated.

"Boys." Ana's tone was full of scorn, and it burned our soft hearts. "Go home. We don't need your help."

Ana was suddenly lit up from the side. All four of the girls turned, and in that moment we knew from the loud rattle of the overstressed engine coming our way that Rafe Torres had discovered his daughters' escape and had tracked them down in his truck.

Hector cried out, "Run!"

But the girls didn't run.

They just waited and watched as their dad honked his horn twice and brought his old green Ford pickup to a stop in the middle of the street. Jessica's heavy suitcase fell to the ground with a thud. Rafe, dressed in a white V-neck undershirt and jeans, jumped from the truck while the engine was still running and went straight for Ana. He gripped her arm, digging his thumb right into her shoulder joint.

"What were you thinking?" he barked. "Huh?"

Ana said nothing. She didn't even wince. She just slowly turned her head to the side, and her gaze slid northward, in the direction of the bus station.

The passenger door of Rafe's truck opened, and out came Hector's mom, wearing fuzzy slippers and a red flannel robe over a long nightgown. She was watching Rafe and Ana with a strange expression on her face. It was a mix of things: like she was relieved, like she was furious, like she was guilty, like she felt sorry for the Torres girls, like she knew, deep down, that it may have been better for them to have caught a bus to the Valley or wherever else they'd hoped to go than to stay with their sad dad in Southtown.

Hector's mom then turned toward us. She ticked up her chin and pointed down the street.

"Walk," she commanded.

We walked. The last thing we saw before we were again swallowed by the noisy, sweaty Fiesta crowd was

Jessica arguing with her father, refusing to get in the truck. If anyone else had noticed what was happening between the Torres girls and Rafe, they didn't let on; everyone knew families were complicated and that dads were always dealing with unruly teenage daughters. Rafe gripped Jessica's arm, then her waist, and then pushed her into the extended cab. She managed to pin us with one more stare, full of hot fury. We deserved it.

We learned on the walk back what had happened. Hector's mom had heard us leave. It took her a minute to figure out what was happening and then to get up and wrestle on her robe. Once she got out into the front yard, she saw Ana's wide-open second-story window. She went across to the Torres house and rang the doorbell until Rafe answered, still half asleep. Together, in Rafe's truck, they drove around the neighborhood, searching for their runaways. At the time, Rafe didn't seem all that mad, Hector's mom told us. Instead, he seemed scared. His fingers were trembling against the steering wheel. He kept repeating, "My girls. My girls." He kept asking Hector's mom, "What will I do if they leave me?"

This is how we learned that we were the ones who had destroyed the Torres girls' chance at escape. If it weren't for us, things would've turned out differently. If it weren't for us, Ana wouldn't have died two months later and her sisters wouldn't have been forced to suffer at the hands of her angry ghost.

Iridian
(Sunday, June 9th)

THE ROUTINE ON Sunday was simple. Rosa got up first. She'd shower, dress for church, and then go out into the backyard for an hour or so and try to talk to the animals. Jessica got up next. The first thing she'd do, even before using the bathroom, was check on Dad. Knowing him, he'd probably have gotten home just as the sun was coming up and would sleep well into the afternoon. After going downstairs to peek into his room, Jessica would head back upstairs and get ready to go to work, which usually took a while, given that she never left the house without looking flawless. Jessica's Sunday shift at the pharmacy didn't start until 11 a.m., but before that she'd pick up her boyfriend John from his house a couple of blocks away so they could go get breakfast somewhere.

Iridian had nowhere to be, so she got up last.

On this particular Sunday, which she hoped would be the same as every other Sunday, Iridian got dressed and went downstairs to the kitchen. After pouring some cereal—chocolate puffs, her favorite—she hopped up on the counter so she could have a better view of Rosa, who was sitting on a wooden chair in the middle of the backyard, facing away from the house. When Rosa wasn't outside, her long hair was the blandest shade of tree-bark brown, but in the sun, especially the morning sun, it was an array of earth tones: pecan, rust, russet.

Rosa's hands were resting on her lap. Her palms were facing up. The light morning breezes tugged at the folds of her faded red dress and the gleaming strands of her hair.

Next door, Mrs. Moreno was out watering the cherry tree she'd just planted. She was frowning at Rosa but also at the Torreses' backyard. It had always been more dirt than grass, and in a corner close to the alley was a pile of mangled metal—the bent carcass of a swing set, the remains of a trampoline, and the rusted frame of a trundle bed. Eventually, Mrs. Moreno realized that Iridian was spying on her spying. Their gazes caught, and Iridian raised her hand to give the older woman a wave. Mrs. Moreno's upper lip stuck on dry teeth in her attempt to smile. As she turned away, the arc of water from her hose swung from the cherry tree to a sorry-looking rosebush that was losing its battle against summer.

Iridian watched as Rosa's shoulders lifted, then lowered. It was a tiny, almost imperceptible movement: a sigh. Iridian saw that little sigh every Sunday morning, and every Sunday morning, it killed her. The day had just started, but already Rosa was disappointed. She woke up full of hope only to have that hope punctured.

Iridian was shoveling in another spoonful of cereal when Rosa stood, dragged her chair back to the porch, and came inside.

"Any luck?" Iridian asked, as the screen door bounced in its frame.

Rosa shook her head and ran her hands over her dress to try to smooth out the creases. She may have been the youngest Torres sister, but Rosa dressed as if she were older—older, like from another century. She wore the same thing every day: a thrift-store dress and bulky brown oxfords. The dresses were short-sleeved, with hems that went at least to her calves, and were buttoned all the way down the front. They reminded Iridian of the kind of clothes that women in Depression-era photographs wore, more fit for standing in a bread line than going to church.

"There was nothing," Rosa replied. "For a second I thought there might have been something, but . . ."

Out in front of the house, a car honked its horn.

"Tell Walter and Mrs. Mata hello," Iridian said.

The Matas had been Rosa's ride to church every Sunday for a year. Walter was a year and a half older than Rosa, and they'd gone all through elementary school and junior high together. The Torres sisters' neighbors and parents of classmates had all taken on various roles—there were bringers of casseroles and mowers of lawns. Mrs. Mata had become transporter to church. The rest of the Torres family stopped going to regular mass soon after Ana died, but Rosa's faith remained big enough for all of them. At Ana's vigil, their old priest Father Canty told Rosa she was special—"full of God" or "touched by God," something like that. He'd insisted Rosa had a purer heart than most people. It was a gift that needed to be nurtured, honed, and then put to use. According to the old priest, if Rosa tried very hard and was very patient, she could see into the hearts of God's creatures, especially those that were small and in need of care. He said her purpose in this life was to soothe the suffering of others.

Father Canty died in his sleep exactly two weeks after Ana's funeral, so he was never able to guide Rosa any further down her spiritual path than that. His replacement was a much younger man, Father Mendoza, who, shortly after arriving to town, got in a fistfight with the still grief-stricken Rafe Torres in the produce section of the grocery store and swore he'd never come near the family again. Iridian was fine with that—she'd fallen asleep during mass for as long as she could remember; the droning words of the sermon softly bounced off her head, never finding their way in—and Jessica had never liked priests because she'd always hated old men telling her what to do. Jessica thought Father Canty's message to Rosa meant that she should volunteer at the children's hospital or the food pantry. Rosa, though, interpreted creatures "small and in need of care" as the animals around the neighborhood, and her sisters eventually just went with it.

"Dad's not in his room," Jessica declared, entering the kitchen and pinning her name tag to her shirt. "Mrs. Mata's outside, Rosa."

The horn sounded again, and Rosa blinked, like she'd briefly forgotten where she was.

"I can't find my keys," Rosa said. "But you'll be here all day, right, Iridian?"

"That's the plan."

Rosa fluttered away, out of the kitchen and through the living room. Once the front screen door clicked shut, Iridian turned to her older sister. Jessica's work uniform consisted of a blue collared shirt and khakis, and it was obvious she'd gone the extra mile that morning to try to offset the unflattering clothes she was forced to wear. Long, loose curls fell down past her shoulders. She smelled like burned hair and aerosol. Her eyes were rimmed with black pencil, and her lips were painted a deep plum color.

"There's cereal if you want some," Iridian said.

"Did you hear me? Dad's not in his room. He won't answer his phone, either." Jessica paused. "I'm worried about him—because of today."

Because of today.

Iridian knew, despite how hard she might hope, that this Sunday wouldn't be like all the other Sundays. That was because this Sunday was June ninth, a year to the day her sister Ana had fallen to her death from her window. Iridian had woken up sick in her sadness—even if *sadness* didn't come close to describing the deep, persistent gnawing that she felt. Emotions were hard for Iridian. She liked to read about them in books, but hated when they crept and settled in her own bones. They made her edgy. They made her sweat. Over the course of the last year, she'd convinced herself she'd gotten really good at ignoring them, brushing them aside, dodging them like a car swerving around a dead animal in the road.

"Dad stayed out." Iridian swallowed a mouthful of now-soggy chocolate globes. "He probably met some fine lady last night and—"

"Stop." Jessica put up her hand and then snatched her car keys off the kitchen table. "I get it. Just let me know when you hear from him, alright?"

Once Jessica was gone, Iridian finished the last of her breakfast, drank the milky dregs, and put the bowl in the sink. Upstairs in her room, she climbed under the covers, then reached under her pillow for her favorite book, *The*

Witching Hour by Anne Rice, which she was just starting again even though she'd already read it over a dozen times. The paper cover had fallen off and was now rubber-banded to the rest of the pages. Iridian could practically recite entire paragraphs by memory, especially the sexy parts between Rowan and Lasher, the ghost that, for centuries, had plagued the women of the Mayfair family, women who also just so happened to be witches.

It was the greatest book ever written.

Bleary-eyed, Iridian looked up to her doorway. She could've sworn she heard someone coming up the stairs and calling her name, but no one was there. She blinked and then glanced at the clock on her nightstand. It was 2:05 in the afternoon. She'd been reading for over four hours. Her right arm was asleep from the elbow down because she'd been lying on it weird.

The front door opened with a high, quick whine.

"Iridian! *Iridian!*"

It was Rosa. She was shouting. Something was wrong. Rosa *never* shouted. Iridian bolted down the stairs and saw her sister standing at the front door.

"It's Dad," Rosa said breathlessly. "In the street."

Iridian pushed past her sister. She was out of the house and running—across the front yard; across Mrs. Moreno's yard, where the water from the sprinkler was creating little suspended prisms in the sunlit air; down the sidewalk; under the shady canopies of the oak trees; and then out into the middle of the street. Down at the intersection, there was a jumble of cars facing every which way.

Iridian's heart lurched, then sank. She was thinking, *There's been a wreck.* Her dad must've been out drinking. Less than a block away from the house, he must've run his truck through a stop sign and into another car, or a couple of cars, or worst of all, a kid out on her bike.

Jessica's old white Civic was there, too, in the middle of the road, with the driver's-side door flung open. She must've been coming home from work on a break. For a panicked moment Iridian was convinced that *she* was the one Rafe had hit.

All around Jessica's car were other cars. The people in them were honking their horns, shouting, waving their arms out the window; but what they *weren't* doing was moaning in pain or calling for help.

Iridian wove through the cars and saw Jessica—her dark hair and the blue of her work shirt. She was crouched down in the intersection next to their dad. He was sitting in the middle of the road in his work coveralls. Sitting and sobbing.

"My girl!" he wailed. "My beautiful girl!"

Jessica had her arms around her dad's shoulders and was talking to him, trying to calm him down, but he didn't seem to realize she was there. Behind them, the green Ford pickup was parked at a diagonal, taking up most of the intersection. Its driver's-side door was open. The engine was still running, so Iridian went over and yanked the keys from the ignition.

"My baby." Rafe collapsed to the side, his face landing hard against the hot asphalt. He closed his eyes. Iridian thought that maybe he'd passed out, but then he curled himself into a ball and started muttering to himself.

"Christ," Jessica said. "Shit, shit, *shit*."

A long stripe of blood was on the road close to the Ford's front bumper, but from what Iridian could see of her dad's hands, legs, arms, and face, he wasn't hurt.

"Iridian!" someone yelled. "Get your father and his truck out of the damn road!"

Iridian turned, grateful for the distraction. Old Mr. Garza was in his idling pickup on the other side of the intersection. His wife was in the passenger seat. They were both dressed for afternoon mass. Mrs. Garza's arms were folded across her chest, and she was giving Iridian her very best, most judgmental glare.

Just beyond the Garzas' truck, a flash of red caught Iridian's eye. It was Rosa. She'd run into the yard of a nearby house. Iridian watched her sister land on her knees in front of a large wheat-colored dog. The dog was on its side, breathing fast. Rosa put her hand gently on its body, against its rib cage, and when she pulled it away, there was blood—blood from the dog, blood on the street.

Rosa looked up—to Iridian, and then past her sister and around. Iridian followed the direction of Rosa's gaze and saw that the entire neighborhood had come out to witness the hideous spectacle of the Torres girls and their father. There were the Matas. Mrs. Moreno. The Johnsons. The Avilas. Hector Garcia from across the street and the boys who hung out at his house all hours of the day and night. Teddy Arenas was in his driveway, leaning against his perpetually broken-down Dodge Charger and drinking a beer. Even Kitty Bolander, the little girl Ana used to babysit, had come up on her bike.

Iridian closed her eyes and gulped, trying to calm down and also magically will the day to start over. When she opened her eyes, there was Rosa again. Her hands were back on the dog. She'd tossed her hair over one shoulder and was lowering her ear against the animal's side. It was only a matter of seconds before Iridian saw the dog shudder, all the way from its nose to the tip of its tail, as if a current had passed through it.

In that same moment, Rafe mumbled, "Ana, my heart."

Sirens bleated in the near distance, which meant that someone had called 9-1-1. Even more people had come out of their houses or stopped their cars along the side streets, attracted to this awful scene like flies on a fresh kill. They were all murmuring, buzzing. Iridian tried to take a big breath in, but the air was thick with exhaust. She erupted into a coughing fit.

"Dad, come on!" Jessica pled. "You *have* to move. Iridian, help!"

Jessica stood and started tugging on Rafe's limp arm. She was crying. The once-perfect black rims around her eyes were blurred. The waves in her hair had flattened. She was yelling at the people in their cars to stop honking their horns and *shut up*.

"Dad, please!" she gasped. "Iridian, do something. *Help me!*"

Iridian didn't help. She didn't move. Instead, she looked back at Rosa, who had left the dog in the yard and was now taking slow steps into the road.

Kitty Bolander's mom was calling out her daughter's name. When she finally reached her, she started to steer Kitty in the direction of home, but then stopped and put her hand on Iridian's shoulder.

"I'm so sorry," she said. "I know this day must be so hard for your family, especially your poor father."

Mrs. Bolander was probably being sincere. Most everyone there probably felt genuinely sorry for Iridian and her family, but that didn't make things any better. If anything, it made Iridian feel like the air was thinning out even more, like all these supposedly well-intentioned people were stealing it from her.

"Iridian!" Again, Mr. Garza honked his horn. "Rafe! Vámanos, man!"

Rafe couldn't hear Mr. Garza. Rafe was lost. He was

still crying, moaning about the pain in his heart and his lost, beautiful daughter. At last, he lifted his bleary gaze to Iridian, and for a moment, they stared at each other. He looked terrible, ill. There were bags around his eyes, large and swollen. His hair, usually pomaded and carefully slicked back, was stuck into spikes as if he'd been trying to yank it from his scalp.

His lips slid against each other. They puckered. He was trying to tell Iridian something, but he couldn't get any words out. That was fine, because Iridian didn't want to hear whatever it was he had to say. All she wanted was to get out of there.

"Rosa," she croaked.

Rosa, the sister whose heart was crafted to ease the suffering of others, came forward, linked her arm with Iridian's, and steered her away. When they were knitted together like this, Iridian felt safer. She didn't even care about the dog's bright blood transferring from Rosa's skin onto hers.

"I think I might've felt it," Rosa whispered excitedly, as the two of them turned back to the house. "Its spirit."

"Where are you two *going*?" Jessica cried out, her voice going shrill. "Iridian, what the fuck? You can't just leave me here with him!"

But that's exactly what Iridian was doing. She didn't even spare a glance over her shoulder.

"Iridian!" Jessica shouted. "Rosa! *Get back here!*"

"I hate him," Iridian said to Rosa, quietly, so only her sister could hear.

"I know."

"We loved her, too. It's like he's forgotten that."

Rosa didn't reply. The sisters kept walking, just the two of them, at a slow and steady pace back to their house.

"I hate him," Iridian repeated. "He doesn't deserve our help."

"I know," Rosa said.

"Iridian!" Behind them, Jessica was nearly hysterical. *"You fucking coward!"*

"Don't pay attention to her." Rosa leaned in. "Maybe just try to walk a little faster?"

Jessica
(Monday, June 10th)

JESSICA REALLY HAD to hand it to her dad. He always tried so hard to make his apologies appear convincing. There was the way he'd start off by looking each of his daughters in the eye, but then duck his head down real quick as if he were just so overcome with emotion. Or there was the way the sides of his mouth would dip into a big-ass frown, the exaggerated kind that a clown would paint on his face. Or there was his voice, how it would get all wobbly, like a kid who tripped on a curb but wanted you to think he was pushed off a building or some shit.

"Girls, listen," Rafe said, staring down at the surface of the kitchen table. He'd even gone the extra mile and shaved that morning. A white strip of dried foam clung to his earlobe.

"I'm so sorry. I didn't know how I'd be when yesterday came around, and I wasn't myself. As you saw." He paused, took a breath, shook his head slowly, and started running his pointer finger down a long gouge in the wood. "You girls are my everything. You know that."

Jessica couldn't help it. Her lower lip started to quiver.

Iridian sat across the table with her arms folded, scowling at Jessica and scowling at Rafe. Rosa was also there, but she was distracted by something out in the backyard.

"Do you see?" Rosa said softly. "It's—"

"I try to be a good father." Rafe's voice broke as he interrupted Rosa. "I *am* a good father, verdad?"

"Yes," Jessica replied, automatically.

Rafe reached across the table for Jessica's hand, and she let him take it. Iridian made a sound, a little cluck of disgust that their dad didn't register.

"This year—" He squinted at Jessica with bloodshot eyes. "This year will be different. I'll change. I promise. I have a plan."

Jessica nodded, but the thing was, he'd said this exact same thing before, almost exactly one year ago.

After Ana died, and after a brief but catastrophic mourning period, Rafe had emerged from his bedroom one day in the middle of July and had made a plan. To his credit, he'd short-term stuck to that plan. He'd gotten up early on Saturday mornings and helped the neighbors fix their cars and their fences and let them use his truck to haul away bulk trash. He didn't go to the bar so much. He paid back a guy that he worked with who had lent him some money. He'd taken Rosa to church, and then to lunch, and then to the art museum. He'd bought Iridian a book. He'd told Jessica to invite a couple of her friends over for a cookout. He'd grilled up hot dogs and cobs of corn. They'd had an okay time.

It didn't last, though. By the end of summer, he was back to his old ways, breaking all kinds of promises. He said he was going to take his girls out for pizza, and then he forgot. He said he was going to be right over to give Jessica's car a jump and then never showed up. Strange dudes started calling at all hours, asking to speak to Rafe, and then made Jessica and her sisters take down messages about "debts" and "payment for services rendered." Those dudes had all said something like, "He knows what we're talking about." A couple of them, before they'd hung up, had asked the girls how old they were.

Back at the breakfast table, Rafe coughed without covering his mouth.

"Are you sick?" Jessica asked. "Do you want me to bring you something from work?"

He shook his head and gave her hand a squeeze. His palm, was it too warm?

"I'm alright."

"Are you sure? It's not a prob—"

"You should go, Dad," Iridian said, interrupting. "It's already after eight. You don't want to be late again. Remember what you told us? About your boss? No more warnings."

"Uh, right." Rafe cleared his throat, removed his hand from Jessica's, and checked his watch. "Right. Jessie, just give me a minute."

He pushed his chair back from the table and went to his bedroom. The police had shown up the previous day, but since a sobriety test had proven Rafe wasn't drunk and no one had actually seen him hit the dog, no charges had been filed. Still, Jessica was worried about her dad behind the wheel—for everyone's sake—so that morning she'd hidden his keys and offered him a ride.

"We all know how you feel about him, Iridian," Jessica said, once their dad was out of earshot. "You could make it a little less obvious."

"He's awful," Iridian snapped. "He's awful, and he doesn't deserve our comfort or your hand-holding."

Jessica wiped away the tear that was threatening to spill from the corner of her eye, and her finger came away smudged black from her eyeliner.

Iridian snickered. "I can't believe you shed tears for that man."

"Like you're so fucking perfect," Jessica replied.

Iridian shoved away from the table, the legs of her chair

squealing against the linoleum floor. She stalked into the living room, turned on the television, and started to flip through the channels.

Rosa moved her chair so that she could sit facing Jessica. She then lifted her fingers up to her sister's face to smooth out the eyeliner. The rising sun coming in from the windows lit Rosa up from behind. In that light, she was weirdly pale. Her eyelids, nostrils, and the upper crest of her ears were practically translucent. Jessica closed her eyes and took a deep breath. Rosa's skin was cool, and the light pressure of her fingers was soothing.

Out in the living room, Iridian landed on what sounded like the local news. With her eyes still closed, Jessica listened for updates about the weather. Overnight there'd been another thunderstorm. Hurricane season had come early that year. Even this far inland, they'd been hit with bad storm after bad storm.

Jessica heard updates, but they weren't about the weather.

> . . . *already at least a couple of sightings near*
> *Concepcion Park. If you see the animal, please*
> *don't approach it. Do not attempt to feed or*
> *capture it. Instead, call police immediately . . .*

"Iridian!" Rosa called out. "What is it?"

"What is *what*?"

"The animal that escaped. What is it?"

Iridian took a couple of seconds before replying. "A spotted hyena. It escaped from the zoo yesterday morning. Those things are gross. They eat babies."

"They do *not* eat babies," Jessica said.

"They do," Iridian insisted. "They come into people's houses at night, steal the little babies, and eat them. I read about it."

"Did the storm wake you last night?" Rosa asked Jessica, giving the corner of her sister's eye one last dab with her finger.

"Yeah," Jessica replied, "I thought the thunder might break my window."

"Ready, Jessie?"

Jessica opened her eyes. Rafe was standing in the entrance to the kitchen. That little crust of foam was still there on his ear, and Jessica's traitor heart clenched at the sight.

"Ready," she said.

The air-conditioning in Jessica's car had been broken for months, so she always kept the windows rolled down while she drove. It was hard to have a conversation or listen to the radio because the wind and the street noise drowned everything out. This meant Jessica couldn't really talk to her dad as she drove him across town to the factory, where he had a job building cars on an assembly line. The silence was fine with her.

Jessica pulled into the lot and let the car idle as her dad climbed out of the passenger seat. After shutting the door, he leaned in through the open window and clasped his calloused hands together. He really did look bad. The sunlight made it worse.

"Jessie. Keep the faith for your old man, huh?"

Jessica smiled. She imagined it looked unconvincing.

"And don't worry about coming to get me later." Rafe gazed up, squinting into the sun. The fingers on his right hand twitched. Jessica worried that he was going to try to reach for her hand like he did earlier at the kitchen table, but he didn't. "I'll figure out a way back. Catch the bus, find a ride or something."

Jessica's phone buzzed in her cup holder. She glanced down to see several missed messages—calls and texts— from John. She'd never heard any of them come in.

Her smile—convincing or otherwise—disappeared completely.

Iridian
(Monday, June 10th)

IN THE WEEKS following their sister's death, the Torres girls would play a game called Who Loved Ana Most. Iridian would always win because she was the best at remembering small details. For example: Ana's left eye sat a little lower on her face than her right. There was a freckle on the inside of her right wrist, at the pulse point. There was a spot on the crown of her head where gray hairs would always sprout. Iridian knew about that last thing because sometimes Ana would ask her to sit up on the bathroom counter and pull those hairs out with tweezers. Ana's favorite movie was *The Princess Bride*, but she'd tell people it was *The Craft*. When she was thirteen, Ana decided she wanted to be a majorette, not because she had school spirit—she didn't—but because the girls' mother was once a majorette, and, most of all, because Ana liked the idea of going out on a great big football field and being the only one of her kind.

The grand prize for Who Loved Ana Most was her room, her clothes and shoes, her makeup, her hairbrushes, and the ancient pack of cigarettes she kept hidden behind the stack of towels in her bathroom cabinet. Jessica, though, kept crying about losing (shocking!), so Iridian caved and gave most of her winnings—Ana's room, Ana's clothes—to her older sister. One night, Iridian spied on Jessica sitting on the edge of the bathroom sink. She had on one of Ana's long, ratty T-shirts and a pair of her old underwear and was wearing her bright pink lipstick. She was leaning against the frame of the open window, trying to mimic Ana's far-off, dreamy look. Iridian hid behind the door and watched Jessica smoke four stale cigarettes, one right after the other. She was puckering her lips so that a perfect hot-pink O would form on the filter. Later, after Iridian had gone back to her room, she could hear her sister throwing up from all the way down the hall. Sometimes Jessica tried too hard.

When Iridian decided to let Jessica have most of Ana's old room, she had one condition: She would get to keep Ana's collection of romance novels, all of which Ana had arranged in three three-foot stacks at the back of her mess of a closet, with the spines facing the wall so that the titles were hidden. It was obvious that most of them had been stolen from the library because they still had the yellowing call slips in them, and because their covers were soft and curled from being read hundreds of times by hundreds of different ladies. The responsible thing would've been to return Ana's books to the library, but Iridian didn't do that. Instead, she carried them all to her room and arranged them the same way Ana had arranged them—in three stacks at the back of her closet, spines facing the wall.

It took a few months to read Ana's old novels, and when Iridian was done, she had a clear sense of her purpose in life: She decided that she wanted to write her own book—a slightly disturbing kind of romance with a slightly disturbing kind of ghost or witch or were-person as the love interest. She had several notebooks full of ideas. She'd brainstormed possible character names: Leticia or LaTisha or Letisha, Gabriel, Viridiana, Sam. She had character descriptions: long chestnut hair, curly auburn hair, crow-black hair, eyes like clear pools, earth-toned skin, freckly skin, freckles that danced across skin, membranous wings, glistening fangs, delicate fingers, scents like clove, lemon, cinnamon, and other things found in a hot tea bag. She'd come up with hundreds of lines of witty banter, and had drawn out intricate family trees featuring the offspring of humans and nonhumans. She'd written out page after page of what it felt like to have body parts come in contact with other body parts, and how that contact would result in gasps, moans, twitches, and full-body shudders. The main characters in most of Ana's novels were fair-skinned and had corn-silk hair that gleamed in the sun, but in Iridian's, the heroines all had hair and skin in various shades of brown.

There was only one book of Ana's that Iridian didn't keep: a school copy of Shakespeare's *King Lear*. It not only had Ana's writing in it—Iridian could tell it was Ana's because of the way she wrote her *a*'s, typed-style with the curl on top—but layers and layers of other students' notes and highlights. Most of the pages were dog-eared and smelled like other people's houses, like cat litter and corn. Iridian wasn't interested in reading a story about daughters and their father—it was a story she lived every day. She took the book back to the school, handed it to Ana's former teacher, and that was that.

After spending the day finishing her reread of *The Witching Hour* in a mostly empty house, Iridian opened her notebook and clicked her pen. Just as she was about to start a conversation between a witch and vampire who were falling in love despite a multigenerational curse, she heard someone coming up the stairs. She knew who it was because the steps were too slow to be Jessica's and too heavy to be Rosa's. Iridian slammed her notebook shut and crammed it into the space between her bed and the wall. She then barreled across her room and braced herself against the doorframe.

"You're not supposed to be here," she said, barring her dad's entrance. "Did you get fired?"

"No, I did not *get fired*, Iridian," Rafe sneered. "My boss let me come home a couple of hours early."

Rafe worked twelve-hour shifts on the line, which meant he shouldn't have been home until after 9 p.m. Iridian glanced at her clock. It was only 5:30.

"More than a couple," she said. "You're not allowed up here."

Rafe towered over his daughter. It was obvious he'd been crying again. It was too dim to see if his eyes were red, but his eyelids were puffed. His gaze swept the darkened room that Iridian and Rosa shared, taking in the two unmade beds, the carpet that hadn't been vacuumed in months, the clothes thrown all over the place.

"Where's your sister?" he asked.

"I don't know." Iridian paused. "Which one?"

"Your *little* sister."

Rosa hadn't been home since the morning, but Iridian wasn't worried. Rosa was a wanderer, had been since she'd been able to walk.

"You're not allowed up here," Iridian repeated.

"This is my house," Rafe replied. "I can go anywhere."

"What do you want?" Iridian felt her fingers dig into the doorframe. She never would've considered herself brave, but she was ready to use her long, weak limbs to defend the contents of her room.

Again, Rafe peered over Iridian's shoulder.

"I'm wondering if you have anything of Ana's," he said. "Anything that I could have."

"Why? What for?"

Rafe waited a moment. "Do I need a reason?"

"Yes," Iridian said, even though she didn't need or want to hear that reason. It wouldn't matter. It probably had to do with missing Ana and wanting a keepsake, a scrap of something that used to belong to her.

He didn't even need to be there, upstairs and lurking. The whole house was still full of Ana's things. Just last week, Iridian had found one of Ana's hairs bundled up in a pair of socks. She knew it was hers because it was long and dark, with about an inch of gray at the root. She'd squeaked with glee when she'd found it, and then wedged it between a couple of pages of *The Witching Hour* like a macabre little bookmark.

"Are you hiding something?" Rafe asked.

"Probably," Iridian shot back. "Get out of my door."

Rafe leaned forward. Lamplight hit his face, and Iridian could see the pink lines from where recent tears had tracked down his cheeks. They looked like burn marks. They did not make her feel sorry for him.

"You girls don't understand," Rafe said.

Iridian said nothing.

"You girls don't *understand*," Rafe repeated. He braced his weight against the doorframe and then dropped his head, shook it.

Iridian couldn't stand this, how her dad always turned his grief into a performance piece.

"You have *no* idea what it's like," Rafe said. "Ana was my heart."

Oh, Iridian had *some* idea what it was like. For her, Ana was hardly even gone. She was everywhere all the time. She was in the walls. She was in the wood of the walls, the wood of the cabinets, the cheap porcelain of the family's mugs, the loops of the terry-cloth hand towels they used to dry their faces, the threads of the worn sheets they slept beneath at night, the pages of the books all stashed in Iridian's closet. She was in the tiniest details of the ways in which the Torres sisters lived their lives, the choices they made, the directions in which they steered themselves, the shades of lipstick Jessica wore. Ana was the one who told Rosa, long before Father Canty ever did, that she was full of magic, that she was different and had a heart that was better-crafted than most people's.

Sometimes, Iridian felt like Ana was the itch in her skin, like she breathed in pieces of her, and then breathed out pieces of her. She cycled through and through. It was overwhelming. Sometimes, like in that very moment, it was too overwhelming. And when things got too overwhelming, Iridian wished she could just shut herself down.

"Your sister died," Rafe said slowly, "because she was keeping secrets."

God, she hated him. Her hate was a sour film coating the back of her throat.

"My sister *died*," Iridian countered, just as slowly, "because she was trying to get away from *you*."

She stepped back into her room and tried to slam the door, but Rafe was too quick and caught it. His other hand whipped out and wrapped around Iridian's upper arm.

"Apologize," Rafe demanded.

"No!"

"You're a miserable girl. Because you're a miserable girl you try to make everyone else miserable."

Maybe that was true—but was it possible that Rafe thought Iridian was the *only* miserable girl in his house?

"You spread your misery," Rafe hissed, squeezing harder. "You're like a disease."

Iridian wrenched her arm free, slammed her door, and bolted it from the inside. She then braced herself there, with both palms and her forehead pressed against the wood, ready for her father to kick the door down or otherwise try to force his way in. She breathed in and out, inhaling the particles of the paint on the door, the particles of Ana. Eventually, Iridian heard Rafe's footsteps receding down the hall. There was a pause and then a slight rattle as he tried the knob on Jessica's locked door. Then there were more steps, hard and heavy, as Rafe went down the stairs.

Iridian counted to one hundred, and then to one hundred again. The weak limbs she would've used to fight her father started to feel even weaker, like foam. Just blow on her and she'd scatter. Once she was fairly certain that her dad wasn't going to come back, Iridian raced to her bed, reached for her notebook, and smacked it to her chest. She was used to her dad throwing out all kinds of insults: little ones that barely pricked and big ones that were meant to crack bone. The best ones were the ones Iridian could snatch out of the air and then save for later, when she'd make them her own. If she could take Rafe's words—no matter how hard or hurtful they were—and write them in her own hand, it transferred their power and made her feel less insignificant. Iridian needed that, to feel less insignificant.

She reached for her pen and opened to a fresh page.

You're like a disease, she wrote.

Jessica

(Monday, June 10th –
early Tuesday, June 11th)

"IT ATTACKED A little boy in his own front yard, then ran off with one of those pequeño dogs," the older woman said. "What kind is that?"

"A Chihuahua?" Jessica offered.

"No, no. More fur."

"Uh . . . a Yorkie?"

"Sí, a Yorkie."

"Oh. Well," Jessica said. "Your total is $14.23."

The woman on the other side of the register took out her wallet, handed Jessica a bank-fresh hundred-dollar bill, and then dumped out all her coins on the counter to hunt for exact change. Of course this was happening while Jessica was the only person working checkout, and while there were five other people in line who were starting to get visibly impatient. One of them was rocking side to side, right foot to left foot to right foot, like he had to go to the bathroom. A man holding a baby in a car seat with one hand and a jug of laundry detergent with the other let out a loud sigh. The old lady ignored him, or she didn't hear him. She bent over the counter and squinted, trying to tell the difference between a penny and a moldy dime.

Jessica picked up the intercom. "Backup to the registers."

"I stopped letting out my cat," the lady said, still hunched. "All night he scratches at the back door, but I don't want Hudspeth snatched up by a hyena. Can you imagine?"

A high school–aged girl joined the line. She was trying to hide a pregnancy test in the sleeve of her hoodie and was biting her lip like she was about to burst into tears. An older man walked over to the photo-maker, holding a flash drive and looking confused.

"I'm confused," he called out.

Again, Jessica reached for the intercom, but stopped when she saw Peter Rojas jogging up from the back of the store.

"I can help the next person," Peter cheerfully announced, sliding behind the counter while clipping on his name tag.

"Thanks," Jessica muttered.

"No problem."

During the summer, Jessica rarely saw Peter. He usually worked the overnight shift and was clocking in around when Jessica was clocking out. The old ladies who shopped at the pharmacy *loved* him. They always asked Jessica if he was working even though they knew his schedule by heart. They went out of their way to steer their carts into the aisle where Peter was stocking or to ask specifically for him to reach for items on the highest shelves. He asked them about their surgeries, and they showed him their granddaughters' senior portraits and photos from their quinceñeras. He seemed genuinely sad when they would tell him that another one of their old lady friends had died.

They'd gone to the same school, but since Peter was Iridian's age and had just finished his junior year, Jessica didn't know him well—they'd been in choir together; that was it—but he was one of Hector Garcia's friends, which meant that, when he wasn't at work, he was usually camped out at the house across the street from Jessica's. He'd been there yesterday afternoon, in fact, standing out in the street with the rest of his friends, gawking as Jessica was trying to yank her distraught father off the ground. He'd seen her at her unraveled worst, begging her sisters for help and yelling at the neighbors to leave them all alone.

Standing there behind the registers under the industrial blast of air-conditioning, Jessica could feel her face get hot and the sweat start to gather behind her ears as if she were still outside with her father, crouched and crying on the asphalt.

"Here, let me," Jessica said to the woman. She plucked twenty-three cents from the pile of coins and started sorting them into the register. "You know, it's probably just scared."

"What, dear?" The woman looked up. "Oh, hello, Peter."

"Hi, Mrs. Rivas," Peter replied.

"The hyena." Jessica handed the woman her change with a long ribbon of coupons. "It's probably just scared. Imagine if you were lost and alone in a strange place. I bet that would be pretty scary. You might start to do some weird stuff."

Mrs. Rivas looked from Jessica to Peter, then back to Jessica.

"But you know," Jessica couldn't help adding, "that thing about the Yorkie? It's probably just a rumor. People around here *love* to come up with all kinds of stories."

Mrs. Rivas, once so chatty, was apparently at a loss for words.

"Have a nice day," Jessica said with a grin. "I can help who's next in line."

Jessica ended up pulling a double because a coworker had to leave to take her kid to the emergency room after he accidentally smashed his hand in a car door. Even though she was exhausted, she was grateful for the excuse not to go home. She spent her time stocking toilet paper, thermometers, greeting cards, condoms, diapers, and cotton rounds. She worked the register some more and tried not to judge customers by their purchases. She spent ten minutes helping an older man look up a coupon on his phone, only to tell him that it had expired three months ago. She ate a granola bar and a fruit cup, and drank a cherry Diet Coke alone in the break room. She caught herself humming along to a Celine Dion ballad that was coming through the speakers. She'd worked four shifts a week at the pharmacy for nearly five months now, since the beginning of the spring semester of her senior year, and had probably heard that same song three hundred times.

Sometimes, she really loved how boring her job was.

Late in the night and toward the end of her second shift, Jessica was with Peter again, this time in the vitamin aisle, where they were scanning hundreds of little bottles that were about to go on sale. The two of them worked in silence, which Jessica thought was great, until Peter asked what he must've assumed was a simple enough question.

"So," he said. "How are you doing?"

Jessica paused, her finger hovering over the trigger of her hand scanner.

"Fine. Why?"

"I don't know." Peter shrugged. "After yesterday. Because of yesterday."

What, Jessica wondered, did Peter think the answer to his question could be? Did he want to know how Jessica went to sleep last night clutching one of Ana's old shoes—one of her *shoes*—because the stink from the sole was still there, and so strong? Did he want to know how, earlier today during her shift, when a twelve-year-old girl wanted to buy the same cheap, linen-scented perfume that Ana always used to wear, Jessica sat in silent judgment of the girl's thin, mouse-brown hair and chapped lips and too-wide eyes, as if some little girl was too weird and too unattractive for a four-dollar plastic bottle of perfume? Or did he want to know about how, while Jessica was having sex with John in the back seat of her car the other night, she started crying so loudly and violently that she'd tricked him? John had thought they'd been cries of passion, what he'd been able to pull from her depths, but they'd had nothing to do with him. Her cries were from grief and rage. She'd bitten John hard, on his shoulder, desperate to cause someone else pain.

Jessica resumed scanning. "I don't feel anything. I'm sort of numb about it."

"What about your dad? Is he doing any better?"

"He gets in these moods," Jessica replied, echoing what

her father had said earlier that morning. "I can't really blame him for some of the things he does."

"I remember when Ana died," Peter said. "It was . . . it was *awful*. Your dad's allowed to have a bad day about it. *You're* allowed to have a bad day about it."

Peter was just trying to be nice—Peter *was* nice—but that didn't make his timing any less terrible or his words any less infuriating. Jessica wanted to wail like a fucking banshee because *this* exactly was the problem: Her entire neighborhood knew all the details of her miserable life. Peter knew. Peter's friends knew. Peter's friends' grandparents knew. Mrs. Rivas from earlier today probably knew. Her fucking cat Hudspeth probably knew. They knew about Jessica's dead mother, her dead sister, her alive but destroyed sisters, her total disaster of a dad.

Jessica's phone chimed, and she pulled it from her back pocket to read a message from John.

hey babe! come get me and lets go somewhere! xxoo.

It was 1:06 a.m. Jessica's shift had been over for six minutes.

"I'll finish all this," Peter said, gesturing to the shelves. "It's no big deal. I've got all night."

"Thanks," Jessica murmured.

She turned and rushed down the aisle toward the break room, where she'd stored her keys and her wallet in her locker. She couldn't wait to be alone in her car, to feel the sticky outside air and to drive with her windows rolled down.

Rosa
(early Tuesday, June 11th)

NIGHTTIME WAS PERFECT for listening. There were birds. Mockingbirds. There were dogs. They all howled together even though they were in separate yards. Mostly, there were crickets. It was hard for Rosa to imagine a single cricket's heart, what it looked like or how fast it beat. Dozens of crickets must fill a backyard on a summer night, all with hearts that thump or whoosh in different rhythms. All those hearts fuel all those legs that scrape together. They scrape together to create a song that will bring them a mate.

Rosa was outside, sitting in her chair and listening to the crickets. A new moon, a perfect white circle, was perched just above the telephone wires, and the air was thick. There were probably going to be storms again. Rosa's hair was puffed around her head, and her bare feet sank a little into the still-damp ground. She felt buzzy and full of static.

Something landed on Rosa's shoulder. She opened her eyes and saw a firefly. She watched it launch off her arm, disappear, glow, disappear, glow. She stood and chased after it, which was something she hadn't done in years.

Another firefly blinked, off to Rosa's left. She spun toward it, but then another caught her eye. And then another. The yard was alive with dancing light. The fireflies pulsed and swooped, so silently. It was dizzying, delirious. Rosa didn't know where to turn. She burst out laughing, feeling lost.

Another firefly lit up right in front of Rosa's face, and when she clasped her hands together to trap it, she could feel the insect's wings flutter against her palms. When she released her cupped hands, Rosa watched for a moment as the firefly blinked away in the direction of Concepcion Park, where the news had said the escaped hyena had first been sighted. Was this a sign? She decided it was. She dragged her chair to the back porch and went inside the house.

Iridian was in the bedroom they shared. She'd fallen asleep with one of her notebooks open on her chest. She did that a lot. The digital clock on the nightstand read 1:16 a.m. Rosa grabbed a backpack from her closet, put on a pair of rubber boots, and left.

Down in the kitchen, she gathered up a half-eaten bag of potato chips, an apple, and a granola bar. She filled a thermos with cold water. She noticed that someone had left the freezer door open slightly, so all of the ice had melted and formed a giant puddle on the floor. A couple of flies were bouncing across the puddle's surface, taking sips from the still-cool water. After throwing down dish towels and scooting them up closer to the bottom of the fridge with the toe of her boot, Rosa left through the back door.

The street her family lived on was just four blocks from the San Antonio River and ran parallel to it, so the walk to Concepcion Park didn't take very long. The closer Rosa got to the water, the more the night sounds started to change. The crickets multiplied. There were thousands of them it seemed like, all of them trilling, but there were also the croaks of frogs. Some birds were chirping, but mostly they rustled in the leaves of the trees that lined either side of the river.

The neighborhood was dark and quiet. Only a few houses had their lights on.

Rosa walked up and down the soggy banks of the river and waited for more signs. She hoped to hear the hyena's laugh, or at the very least, a quick huff of its breath. She hoped to see the flash of a glassy eye, something she could follow. It wouldn't have been as bright and clear as the glow of a firefly, but it might be enough.

The water in the river was a rushing murmur, but

occasionally there were pops and plunks, like twigs breaking and falling into the murk. Speakers from a car somewhere out in the neighborhood went *boom, boom, boom*. Rosa couldn't hear the music, just the *boom, boom, boom*.

The perfect circle moon was high overhead when Rosa finally stopped to sit on the ground near the riverbank. She opened her backpack and started eating her apple. Once she was done, she pitched the core into the water and lay down on the driest patch of grass she could find. Resting her head on her backpack, she stretched out and gazed up at the sky. There weren't many stars in the heart of the city, but there were some.

Rosa believed in signs, but she didn't believe in coincidences. It was no coincidence, for example, that the anniversary of Ana's death came on the same day that an animal escaped from the zoo. Maybe other people wouldn't see those two things as linked, but Rosa liked to think that she was more attentive than most people.

She just wasn't quite sure of *how* or *why* those two things were linked yet. She had to be patient and let the answers come to her. Patience was key.

Something buzzed in Rosa's ear, probably a mosquito.

What, she wondered, went on in a mosquito's heart?

Rosa closed her eyes and curled her fingers into the grass. It felt a little bit like fur.

Jessica

(early Tuesday, June 11th)

RAFE HAD A rule against boys in the house, and John shared a bedroom with his brother and his cousin, so Jessica's car was usually the only place where she and John could be alone together. Sometimes they sat in her car outside of John's house. Other times they went to a park or the empty lot of an office building. Sometimes they made out. Sometimes they talked. Sometimes, they made out *then* talked.

For now, they were parked a couple of streets over from Jessica's house, across from the high school. They weren't making out. Or talking. They were just sitting. It was three-something in the morning. Thunderclouds were rolling in, and Jessica was waiting for John to tell her to drive him home.

It had only been a little over two hours since she'd run out of the pharmacy and plunked down with a contented sigh into the front seat of her car. She didn't feel content anymore.

"Aren't you tired?" Jessica asked.

John shifted, angling in. "You're trying to get rid of me?"

John usually smelled like his house, which smelled like his kitchen, which smelled like the yeasty bread his grandmother liked to bake. Tonight, he didn't smell like that. He smelled sour. Not sour like yeast, but sour like sweat, like he'd been out under the sun for hours, sweating then cooling, sweating then cooling.

"Of course I'm not trying to get rid of you." Jessica slouched in her seat. "I'm just tired. I was at the store forever, and I have to get up early tomorrow and go back again. Hey, speaking of that . . . I've been thinking about asking my manager about transferring."

What Jessica said next came out in a rush.

"It wouldn't be for a while. I'd have to make sure my family was set up alright, and I wouldn't go anywhere too far, just like to Austin or Galveston. It's a good time for a new start, you know? You and I—we can get a cheap little place together, but still be close enough to visit home when we wanted."

It took a while for John to respond. "The last time you tried to run away it didn't work so well."

Jessica scoffed. "It's not *running away* if I'm sitting here telling you about it. I'm asking you to come with me."

"I love you, Jess," John said. "But I'm not leaving San Antonio."

"But do you *want* to?" Jessica urged.

"It's not about wanting to or not. I won't leave. My family needs me."

Jessica held in a snicker. John's family needed him for what, exactly? He'd never had a job. His mom spoiled him rotten, and since his car broke down in the spring, all he'd been able to say he'd done this summer was stay home and fix his little cousin grilled cheese sandwiches for lunch every day.

What did John know about a family that needed him? Jessica's dad had turned from a man into a puddle the other day and would've stayed there, sobbing on the street, for God knows how long, if Jessica hadn't literally hauled him off the ground and begged him to walk. When he wasn't having a public meltdown, Rafe required nonstop words of love and loyalty. He also required food, so Jessica had to carve out money from her paycheck each month to keep the fridge stocked. She also had to make sure Iridian didn't fossilize under the covers of her bed and that Rosa didn't do something weird like sprout wings and fly off into the sky.

Speaking of Rosa.

Up ahead, a familiar form wearing a long dress and

rubber boots was crossing the street. As Rosa passed under a streetlight, Jessica noticed she was eating something. Beef jerky? A candy bar?

"Is that . . . ?" John asked.

Jessica honked her horn.

Rosa stopped and turned. She waved and then waited as Jessica started her car and drove up the block.

"What are you doing?" Jessica called out the open window as she pulled up alongside her sister. "It's about to start raining."

Rosa turned toward the black sky pulsing behind her, and as Jessica stuck her hand out the window, she could feel the humidity breaking and giving way to cool, pre-storm winds.

"I know," Rosa replied, taking a bite of what Jessica could now see was a granola bar. She stepped closer to the car, and Jessica saw blades of grass sticking to the fabric of her sister's dress, and mud caking her boots. Rosa was also, for some reason, wearing a backpack. "I was on my way home."

"On your way home from *where*?" Jessica demanded.

"The river," Rosa said, simply. "I was looking for the hyena."

John barked out a laugh.

"Of course you were," Jessica replied. "Just get in the car."

The Day Jessica Torres
Attacked a Priest

HECTOR'S PARENTS, BEING good Catholics, opened their home after Ana's funeral so that the neighbors could gather, pick at potluck dishes, and express their condolences to the thoroughly distraught Torres family. The girls were there, of course. Rosa was wandering around in a somber daze. Iridian was wide-eyed and stunned, and Jessica was looking . . . lost. It was so unlike her. She just shuffled from room to room, her gaze pinned to the floor. She was wearing Ana's lipstick, a dangerous shade of near-hot pink, as well as a bluebonnet-blue sundress that used to belong to her older sister. It was several sizes too big and it swallowed her up.

We were there, too, of course—forced by our parents

to wear our church clothes and to stay downstairs with everyone else and not hide up in Hector's room. That was okay because we were on a mission. We started out in a cluster at the base of the stairs and then fanned out from there. We hovered, eavesdropping, seeking more details about Ana.

On the night she died, we'd all fallen asleep watching television in Hector's room and had woken up to a sound—at first, Jimmy thought it was a gunshot; Calvin said it was more like the hard, sharp beat of a snare drum—followed by a girl's strangled cry. That cry was followed by the hard snap of a tree limb breaking, which was followed by the squeal of tires against the asphalt as a car tore down the street. We tumbled over one another to get to the window. The first thing we saw were Ana's curtains, flapping gently in the summer wind. Her window was open—no, not open, *broken*. Someone must've thrown something through it. We watched a piece of glass the size of a hubcap dangle from the frame, then fall. Then, Ana's sisters appeared in the window. They were screaming.

They were screaming because there, facedown in the yard, at the base of the oak tree, was Ana. Her body was not twisted, her legs and neck not kinked at strange angles, but her long dark hair was fanned out across the dried-out patches of grass, and she wasn't moving. A flip-flop was on her right foot. Its mate was on top of a nearby bush. Clutched in Ana's right hand was a branch from the oak tree, as if she'd tried, at the very last second, to reach out, take hold, and break her fall.

After that, everything happened so fast: Ana's sisters kept screaming, but now they were out in the yard. The ambulance came; the cops came. Rafe was sitting on the porch step with his head in his hands. The neighbors had to run into the yard to console the Torres sisters because it was clear Rafe wasn't going to do it himself.

The official word was that Ana was in the process of sneaking out her window when she lost her footing and fell. As much as we'd wanted to be Ana's heroes and take her away to wherever it was she wanted to go, there were other guys who played that role for her. Several nights a week, various guys—*older* guys, older guys *with cars*—would ease to a stop a couple of houses down the street, turn off their lights, and wait. Eventually, Ana would open her window and climb down the oak tree. She'd run to the car and be off and gone for a couple of hours, and when she'd come back she'd be in a state of sort-of undone: Her skirt would be a little twisted, the hem of it not quite lined up right. Her hair would be ratted in the back.

But there were other theories about Ana's death: she leapt, intentionally, after a fight with her father; she leapt, intentionally, after learning she was pregnant and that the baby's father was an older married guy; she leapt, intentionally, because she was a sad girl trapped in a sad house.

At Hector's, it was hard to watch the Torres girls shuffle

from room to room and politely receive various words of sympathy because we could see the pain in their faces—the pain of their loss and the pain that comes along with forcing small smiles and pretending that kind words from their neighbors made any kind of difference.

In other parts of the house, there was the usual stuff whispered in corners about Rafe being a tragedy of a man. He'd never been the same since his wife, Rita de la Cruz, had died shortly after giving birth to Rosa. He'd become a shell, helpless. He couldn't make the most basic decisions, like what to get for takeout or which shirt to wear to church. For a while, he'd taken up with an older widow from the neighborhood named Norma Galván, and after that had fizzled out, he'd been involved with various other women. He wanted them to take care of him; they wanted to take care of him. Unfortunately, none of them lasted for longer than two months, and, in the end, all he could truly rely on, or so he said, were his girls. In this life, family was all there was.

We heard that he'd told his daughters that if they got jobs, the money would have to go to the family—for groceries, bills, house repairs, stuff like that. Once the girls graduated and if they decided they wanted to keep going to school, it had to be at one of the nearby Alamo Colleges, close enough for them to commute from home.

The weight of Rafe's neediness was heavy enough to crush all four of the Torres sisters, but Ana, being the oldest in a motherless household, bore the brunt of it. She packed her father's lunches for him in the mornings, made sure his Negra Modelos were poured into frosted mugs when he got home, and went to neighbors' houses to try to smooth over bitter feelings after Rafe borrowed money he couldn't repay.

The women gathered in the Garcias' kitchen on the day of Ana's funeral shook their heads—pitiful, they said, patètico. Some said it wasn't his fault, the way he was.

"He was born out of God's favor," Kitty Bolander's mom claimed. "Anda mal. The clouds, they follow him. He walks outside, and it starts to hail."

Father Canty, who'd led Ana's graveside service, hadn't arrived yet, but three other priests from the local parish were there, pinching small paper plates in their large sausage fingers while shoveling down heaping forkfuls of Calvin's mom's famous King Ranch chicken.

The priests didn't notice us lurking nearby. We watched as they spilled sour cream down the front of their robes and dabbed at the little white blurs with their napkins. One of them burped and didn't even say excuse me. The things they were talking about to each other were like the things we heard people say in mobster movies. One said that Rafe was in a *bad spot* and that he owed someone named Edgar Rivera Lopez—we'd never heard of him—a *boatload* of money. The situation had gotten so bad that Rafe was living in a perpetual state of fear. He was *marked*.

Another priest said, "He will be forced to leave San Antonio and go back to Crystal City."

Another added, "He cannot hide forever."

For a moment, the priests were quiet. One of them put his empty plate on a side table and took a long drink from his plastic cup. Then he sighed. "Rafe is overwhelmed," he began, "and was never equipped to raise four daughters on his own. It doesn't help knowing now how rebellious Ana was. It's possible she was also a liar. It's all because she has no mother."

The first priest shook his head and muttered something we couldn't really hear, but by then we weren't listening. Our attention had shifted to Jessica, who'd suddenly and silently appeared in the doorway. From the expression on her face—blanched white with anger, a familiar sight—it was obvious she'd heard everything the priests had said. She opened her mouth to speak just as her dad came up from behind her and gently gripped her shoulder. Iridian and Rosa were behind him. He leaned down, said something into Jessica's ear, and started to steer her away. It was time to go. Jessica left with her words unspoken.

The gathering went on. There was still food to be eaten and rumors to be spread about Rafe's no-good luck and his problems with money and women and life in general, but, in other corners of the house, talk had shifted to the upcoming basketball season and concerns about the neighborhood: rising taxes, petty fines imposed for minor code violations, and families who'd lived in the same house for decades being bought out by developers. There were For Sale signs on almost every street now.

Father Canty finally arrived and joined the huddle of priests. They were on their third helping of King Ranch chicken when Jessica returned. She stormed in through the front door and then right past us, the massive folds of her blue dress swishing around her legs. She smelled like sweat and lawn clippings. She was sisterless, fatherless, alone.

She stopped in front of the group of priests, waiting for them to notice her. When they didn't, she reached out and tugged on the sleeve closest to her. It belonged to the one who had referred to Ana as "rebellious."

That priest turned, and the others did the same. Collectively, they wiped the corners of their mouths with their napkins and shifted their expressions to ones of well-practiced sympathy.

"You didn't know Ana!" Jessica shouted. She spun toward Father Canty. "You didn't know her, so don't talk about her like you did!"

If Father Canty was stunned by the confrontation, he didn't show it. Instead, he stepped forward and bent at the waist so that he was eye to eye with Jessica.

"My dear," he said tenderly, "I know this is a very difficult time for you, but you are a young woman, and as such, you have to consider that there are many things in life you do not yet understand."

Jessica lunged. With an open palm, she hit Father Canty in the face. Then she screamed and raked her nails across his cheek.

Hector's dad rushed forward. He pulled Jessica away, hoisting her into the air, where she continued to kick and thrash, her dark braid whipping around her head. Her dress rode high, exposing the length of her brown legs. Father Canty pressed a napkin against his face and seemed surprised to see, when he pulled it away, that the girl had managed to draw blood.

Jessica was almost through the door of the room when she threw out her hands, gripped the frame, and braced herself there.

"Don't tell me I don't understand!" she screamed. "Ana was not a liar! You're the liar, old man! You!"

Hector's dad was pulling hard, but Jessica wouldn't budge. She turned her head and spit in his eye. She tore the paint from the doorframe the same way she'd torn the skin from the priest's face. Finally, brave Mrs. Bolander went over and pried Jessica's fingers from the doorframe one by one.

"I hate you!" Jessica yelled, as Hector's dad tossed her over his shoulder like a bag of lawn fertilizer and carried her through the front door. "I hate you all!"

We watched through the window, mouths agape, as Jessica Torres was carried across the street to her house. The whole time, she kept kicking and screaming.

If anything, once outside, her screams got even louder.

Jessica
(Tuesday, June 11th)

JESSICA STOCKED BIRTHDAY cards, lip balm, bags of little chocolate bars, whole milk, skim milk, almond milk, soy milk. She worked the register for an hour, and people kept coming in, one right after another after another. She tried to guess what they would buy, and she was right about forty percent of the time. When it came time for her lunch break, Jessica sat in the back room, humming to herself, eating some nearly expired deli meat and cheese she'd bought from the refrigerated section and drinking a cherry Diet Coke. It was all very normal.

• • •

At six-thirty, half an hour after her shift had ended, Jessica was in the parking lot of the pharmacy, sweating through her clothes and staring at the engine of her car. The battery was dead. Her phone was buzzing nonstop in her back pocket. She didn't even need to look to know it was John. She'd told him earlier she'd swing by his place after work to pick him up, and now she was late.

"Oh, *come on!*" Jessica yelled.

"Need a jump?"

Jessica spun around, and there was Peter Rojas, backlit by the sun, looking like a saint holding a pair of jumper cables.

"Yes. A jump. Please. Thanks. We have those at the house, but I always forget to get them out of the garage."

"No problem," Peter replied.

Peter jogged over to his truck to pull it closer. He kept the engine running as he opened the hood and attached the cables, positive to positive and negative to negative. Jessica noticed a bead of sweat trickling down from Peter's hairline to the outside edge of his eyebrow, and she had the strange, sudden urge to swipe it off with her finger.

Once he was done, Peter straightened. He was so tall he blocked out the sun, and Jessica had to tilt her chin up to look him in the eye. For a while, Peter said nothing as he peered down at Jessica with that slightly perplexed expression people get when they're trying to figure out what to say or if they should say anything at all.

Jessica's phone buzzed again. Sweat was pooling at her lower back. She was ready to get this show on the fucking road.

"What?" she urged.

"Nothing."

"No, not nothing. What?"

Peter shifted his weight to lean against the front bumper. "Do you still sing?"

Jessica coughed, thrown by the question.

The answer was *no*, and Peter knew that. Jessica had stopped singing with the school choir the fall after Ana died. Peter had stayed on.

"Why would you ask me that?" she asked.

"It was just a question." Peter shrugged. "I heard you in the break room the other day singing along to some song. It reminded me of when we were in choir together."

"So you were spying on me?"

"We work together, Jessica," Peter replied, deadpan. "I was in the break room. You were in the break room."

"So, you were spying on me."

Jessica understood why everyone liked Peter. Really, she did. He was the epitome of a good egg—the kind of person who carried jumper cables in his truck and helped strangers and was patient with old people. Jessica was a terrible, terribly judgmental, rude and selfish person, and, because of that, Peter and Peter's kindness made her feel even worse about herself than she already did.

"You know what?" Peter said. "Forget it. Forget I said anything."

Jessica snorted. "Right."

Peter gestured to the battery. "You want to get in and give it a try?"

Jessica said nothing as she climbed into her car and twisted the key in the ignition. After a series of sputters, the engine finally caught. She sagged with relief as Peter unfastened the cables and slammed down her hood.

"Crisis averted." He swiped his brow with the back of his hand, leaving behind a smudge of grease. One of the old ladies in the store would spot it later and make a big production of wiping it away.

"Thanks," Jessica muttered through the window.

"You're welcome."

"See you later."

"Great."

"Great."

"Cool."

They were talking like robots now.

Jessica wished Peter would just walk away, but there he was, still with that slightly perplexed expression on his face. Surely he wasn't going to ask her more questions about singing. It was possible he was going to try again to ask some version of the very worst question of all—*How are you doing?*—and Jessica wasn't sure she'd be able to handle it.

"Is everything okay?" Peter asked.

"God, Peter. Everything's *fine*."

By now another little line of sweat had tracked all the way down the side of Peter's face. A bead was hanging there, right at the edge of his jaw. Instead of reaching out and swiping it away like she still wanted to, Jessica began tapping her fingers against her steering wheel.

Peter looked down. The bead of sweat dropped from his jaw to the asphalt and then vanished.

"Okay, well." Jessica shifted her car into reverse. "Thanks again."

Even before she'd pulled all the way out of her parking space, Jessica's phone buzzed, immediately buzzed again, and then started buzzing nonstop. A call was coming in. She ignored it.

When she was about halfway to John's, Jessica pulled over but kept the car running on a side street. She tilted her head back against the seat and started to sing. Just to herself—along with nothing. She began softly, but then got louder and louder. The singing turned to shouting, and Jessica became vaguely aware of a woman walking her dog—one of those pequeño dogs, but neither a Yorkie nor a Chihuahua—who had slowed and kept glancing her direction.

Jessica's phone buzzed again and, finally, she grabbed it. Without even reading the message, she typed out a reply.

Sorry. On way. Manager made me stay late. xo

Jessica hesitated, trying to think of a better way to lie or not-quite lie. She couldn't come up with anything, so she just hit send. She pulled away from the curb, still belting out a song to no one but herself.

What a question: *Do you still sing?*

Peter would never know her secrets.

Rosa

(Tuesday, June 11th)

ROSA'S SEARCHING AT night hadn't yielded any results, so she thought the daytime might be better. It wasn't. She'd spent hours out in the heavy humidity and had found nothing. When she was on her way back, and just a block from her house, she stopped to watch two cardinals swoop through the branches of an oak tree in a neighbor's yard. The birds were spinning in circles, diving into each other, knocking leaves loose. They were a happy tangle of flapping and chirping. Eventually, one of them landed on a branch so thin that it couldn't support its light, hollow bones. The branch snapped. The bird fell. Rosa expected the cardinal to stop itself, do a graceful mid-air pivot, and resume playing with its bird-friend. Instead, it plummeted all the way to the ground and landed without a sound, in the grass. Rosa looked up the street and then down to see if anyone else had noticed, but aside from Teddy Arenas checking his mailbox a few houses away, she was alone. The other cardinal, on a high branch above, waited for a moment, let out a couple of mournful chirps, and flew away. On the ground, a red wing fanned above the blades of grass, motionless.

She'd never seen anything like that before.

Iridian

(Tuesday, June 11th)

IRIDIAN WAS STARING at herself in the mirror. The midday light was good. She was tilting her head—left, right, up, down—to catch the shadows, and putting her fingers on her skin to mash it around. When Iridian was younger, she'd stick Scotch tape all over her face to pull the corners of her lips up or down or to try to flatten out her sharp nose.

She was practicing at becoming invincible. Every day, she'd stand in front of her bathroom mirror and come up with insults to hurl at her reflection. She practiced keeping her expression blank and worked at dodging and deflecting.

"Beakish," she said to herself. "You look like a fucking bird."

It had taken a long time and a lot of practice, but Iridian had gotten pretty close to convincing herself that her face—with eyes set too wide like a lizard's, a nose like . . . well, like a beak, and lips so thin that when she puckered they looked like a wadded-up gum wrapper—had *character*. Most of the books she read had girls in them who weren't beautiful, but whose faces had *character*. This just meant that the things that made them *them* were on the inside. In those stories, it may take a while, but eventually a person would come around who admired those girls for their giant hearts or their razor wit or their unbendable will.

Iridian was leaning forward, her nose practically grazing the mirror, when a thump on the wall behind her caused her to jolt.

"Rosa?" Iridian called.

Her sister didn't respond, so Iridian stuck her head out into the hall. The door to their bedroom was slightly open. There were no lights on, but the sun was shining in through a gap in the curtains. Maybe it was nothing. Maybe there was a squirrel in the attic.

Iridian went downstairs. She sat on the counter and ate cereal for the second time that day. After she was done eating, she rinsed her bowl, went back to her room, and brought one of her notebooks from her hidden stacks into her bed. She picked up a pen and opened to a page in the middle. She'd been making progress on her witch-vampire love story. The plot wasn't really there yet, but she'd been brainstorming some good scenes.

I want him, Iridian wrote. *But above all, I want him to want me. I want him to want me so badly that he'll bury his teeth into the flesh of my arm and tear off a piece of it.*

I like to watch his hands and the way he grips his pen when he scribbles a note to himself, or how, when he sleeps, his fingers still seem to move, knowingly, tapping lightly across the covers. I reach out with my own hand, mimicking the movements across his skin, and he twitches. Sometimes he startles awake.

I want to float into him, for him to absorb me, for him to eat me up.

Iridian wrote and wrote and wrote.

After a while, she heard the sound of her sister's light footsteps coming up the stairs. She looked up to see Rosa standing at the door.

"What's up?" Iridian asked.

"Dad's home."

It was the second time in two days he was home when he shouldn't have been.

"Okay."

"He doesn't look good."

Iridian paused. "And?"

Rosa didn't reply.

"Where's Jessica?" Iridian asked.

This was what *she* did: dealt with Dad.

"Still at work, I think."

Iridian made a big show of throwing down her notebook before following her sister downstairs.

Rafe was on the couch in the living room, bent over and gripping the sides of his head. Rosa was right: He didn't look good. He was grimacing, pressing his fingers against his temples so hard that the tips were going white.

"He's drunk," Iridian said to her sister.

Rosa gave her head a shake. "I don't think so."

Iridian knelt down in front of her dad. He didn't smell drunk, but he sure looked it. He was still folded in half, so Iridian pushed him up to where he was sitting semi-straight. His hands fell limply into his lap, and Iridian's gaze fell to his wrist, around which was a piece of yellow string. Three beads were threaded on it: a white one, a blue one, and a black one. Even though Iridian hadn't seen that bracelet in probably ten years, she recognized it immediately. Ana had made it one day in elementary school, during art class. God only knows where Rafe had found it—probably shoved in the back of a kitchen drawer. Iridian made a noise—sort of like a cluck or a gurgle—and had to look away. She felt sick, actually nauseated, by the sight of a little girl's bracelet on a grown man's wrist.

Rafe coughed a couple of times. He didn't cover his mouth. Usually when he was drunk his face would turn punch red, but this was different. His skin was pale, mottled like a TV-show corpse. He coughed again, then wheezed. He unzipped his jacket partway, revealing the white V-neck shirt beneath. His chest heaved as he struggled to get breath down into his lungs.

"Are you okay?" Iridian asked. "You don't look so great, Dad."

"Too warm," Rafe said.

The AC was blasting, and the ceiling fan was directly overhead, whipping around at what seemed to be a dangerously high speed.

Rafe turned his head and mumbled something to his youngest daughter. Rosa left the room and went into the kitchen, where Iridian could hear the creak of a cabinet door opening, followed by the whoosh of water running from the tap.

"Hey." Iridian poked her dad in the shoulder. "If you're sick I can call Jessica and have her bring something home from the pharmacy, yeah?"

Rosa returned and placed a glass of ice water in her dad's hand. None of the family's glasses were part of a matching set, and some were so old they used to belong to the girls' grandparents. This one once had white-and-yellow flowers painted on it, but by now all the flowers had practically smudged off from years of use.

Rafe took a shaky sip of water, then cleared his throat to get Iridian's attention. When their eyes met, Iridian braced herself for her dad to tell her she was like a disease, or something else equally awful.

He croaked out, "Ana," and then erupted into a coughing fit. Rosa snatched the glass away so that he wouldn't spill and placed it on the coffee table.

Ana. Ana, Ana, Ana.

"Dad, I know—" Iridian started.

"Iridian," Rafe said, interrupting. "I can't breathe . . . my head."

Iridian sighed. Which was it? His lungs or his head?

"We'll call Jessica," Rosa offered. "She can come home and take you to one of those twenty-four-hour clinics."

"I don't need a clinic. No doctors." Rafe groaned and pushed himself to standing. He was up, but wobbly. He placed his hand on the back of the couch. There it was again: that little string bracelet.

A series of soft sounds—a click, a plunk, and a thunk—caused Iridian to turn. The glass Rosa had just placed on the table had tipped, spilling water and ice across the wood surface and down onto the carpet.

"I must've bumped it," Rosa said, rushing to the kitchen for paper towels.

Rafe hobbled into his room and closed the door. Iridian was still on the floor in the living room, sitting on her heels. By then, both of her feet were asleep. Her thoughts went to her closet, to her books, then to her bed, and to her notebook. All she wanted was to spend the rest of this day with those pages.

"I'm going back upstairs," Iridian called out to Rosa. "If he does this again, don't come get me."

Jessica

(early Wednesday, June 12th)

STONES PLUNKED AGAINST Jessica's window. At first, she had one of those moments when dream and reality merge: She was at the pharmacy, opening boxes in the stockroom. Peter Rojas was there with her, and he kept picking up and dropping the same heavy box on the concrete floor over and over again.

Then Jessica was awake, but not all the way. She vaguely realized she was in her bed with the covers pulled up over her head. Her breath caught, and her eyes flew open. She tossed off her comforter, hurled herself across the room, and pulled back the curtains. John was there with his arm cocked back like a baseball pitcher. He grinned as he let a stone fly at Jessica's window. Behind him, idling at the curb, was Jenny Sanchez's Buick.

Jessica hadn't gotten much sleep in the last few days, so she wasn't in the mood for whatever this was. She knew, however, that she couldn't just leave John out there. She held up a hand, telling him to wait, and after wrestling on some clothes—cutoffs, a T-shirt, flip-flops—she crept downstairs.

"What are you doing here?" Jessica whispered to John once she was out in the yard. "What happened to your phone?"

"Dead," John replied. "Come on."

John led Jessica to the car and held the door open. Jessica slid into the back seat, bracing herself for the reek of stale cigarette smoke. John climbed in next to her. Jenny's Buick was a hand-me-down of a hand-me-down. It used to belong to Jenny's brother, and before that, to Jenny's uncle. Its color was a nearly iridescent pale sky blue, and what was left of the original interior—what wasn't patched up with black electrical tape—was royal blue leather. It reminded Jessica of a big metal blue jay.

"Hi, Jenny," Jessica said.

"Hey, girl." Jenny flicked the ash of her cigarette out her open window and reached up to the steering column to shift the car into drive.

John threw his arm around Jessica's shoulders.

"Seriously," Jessica urged. "What are you doing here?"

"C'mon, Jess." John brought her into an embrace that was just a little too tight. "Where's your sense of adventure?"

Jenny drove north, into the heart of downtown San Antonio, and then parked her car on an empty side street. From there, John led Jessica across a large, empty square toward the Cathedral of San Fernando. This was Rosa's church, and the family's church back when they pretended to be Catholics. It wasn't just a church, though. It was more like a monument, an architectural marvel, a mammoth thing built hundreds of years ago with towers and arches and spires and bells that rang to mark the hours.

As Jessica neared this church-monument, she could hear whispers and hushed laughter, but she couldn't yet see who was there. She could only make out dark, body-shaped clouds and phone screens and the glowing tips of cigarettes.

"Hey," Jenny called out. "Sorry we're late."

Heads turned. People said hey back. At this point Jessica could see that the group was made up of people from school or friends of friends, maybe a dozen total, including, of all people, Peter Rojas.

Peter was standing on the fringes, next to Calvin, another one of the boys who was always at Hector's house.

It was weird to see Peter there, out of his element, wearing normal clothes—army green shorts that came just past his knees and a white T-shirt—and without a name tag pinned to his chest. His shoes were the same, though: off-white canvas sneakers, not that Jessica would admit to noticing. Their eyes met, and Peter gave Jessica a small nod before looking away.

"So what's going on?" John asked.

"Okay," Jenny said, pausing to light another cigarette. "We're playing sardines in the church. Someone hides, like in hide-and-seek. The rest of us wait out here for five minutes, then go in. When you find the person who's hiding, you hide with them. The point is for the group of hiders to get bigger and bigger until there's just one person left running around the church wondering where the hell everyone is. So." Jenny looked around, took a drag from her cigarette, and exhaled a puff of smoke into the dark night. "Who's hiding first?"

"Me," Jessica said. "I'll go."

John cocked his head. "Really?"

"Really." Jessica smiled. "Here's my sense of adventure."

"Okay," Jenny said. "Good luck. You have five minutes."

Jessica skipped quickly up the stone steps that led to the entrance of the church and kicked off her flip-flops so they wouldn't suck and slap against the tile. It took both of her hands to open the giant wooden door and shut it behind her, and once inside, she waited for her eyes to adjust to the darkness. Directly in front of her was the font of holy water, and beyond that were the doors that led to the cathedral proper. On either side of her were more closed doors that led to hallways, offices, more rooms—all good places to hide, for sure. The cathedral, though— that's where Jessica wanted to go.

It was dark there, except over to her left where the red glass candles glowed in staggered rows. Jessica remembered the church smelling like blown-out matches and incense, but that night it didn't smell like that. If anything, it smelled like Rosa: clean, comforting, and faintly like dust. Jessica padded down the center aisle, the tile ice cold under her bare feet, and turned down one of the rows.

She could've sat or reclined on the pew, but instead she shimmied beneath it so that she was flat on the floor. The wood of the bench was inches from her face, and just above the tip of her nose was a gray, penny-sized circle of chewed and flattened gum. She took a big breath in and then out and then waited.

It seemed like longer than five minutes before the front doors of the church opened. There were whispers, followed by a bright, loud laugh. Jessica heard everyone go off in different directions, some into the hallways that extended off that front room, others up stairs. The cathedral doors creaked open. Someone was heading over to the side, in the direction of the confession booth. At least a couple of people were coming down the center aisle. Eventually, Jessica saw a pair of beat-up black Adidas coming her way. They were John's. She pushed back deeper under the pew, causing it to squeak. John stopped. He shuffled his feet and turned in a circle. He didn't see Jessica, didn't realize she was there. She could've reached out and touched him. She could've scraped her nail against his rubber sole. If she'd had a pin, she could've pricked the skin of his ankle with it.

"Jess," John hissed, not down to where she was, but out to the whole room. "Jess, babe. Where are you?"

Jessica covered her mouth with her hand. How funny that John thought she would respond to him. He *actually* thought that she wanted him to find her, just like he thought she wanted him to wake her up in the middle of the night and force her out of bed, but he didn't know how thrilled she was to be left alone in the cold dark. Now that she had that thrill, she wanted to hold on to it, coat it in sugar and chew on it.

John whispered a curse and then took off down the row toward the center aisle. Back at the door, he stopped and called out again. Jessica didn't respond. She still had her hand over her mouth. Eventually, the doors opened, John's footsteps faded, and the cathedral was quiet. Jessica exhaled and laughed to herself.

The quiet didn't last very long. Little by little, the cathedral filled back up with sound. Pipes started to bang.

The floorboards up in the organist's loft creaked as if someone was slowly pacing back and forth across them. Voices rose up from other sections of the church, the sound seeping through the cracks of the stone. There were echoes and the click-clack of shoes against tile.

Jessica could explain away the creepy sounds. The banging noises could be from an old boiler. The groans could be from the centuries-old foundation continuing to settle. That or rats. What sounded like ghosts talking to each other was most likely wind or the voices of Jessica's not-really friends being carried through the pipes.

Jessica had never been afraid of the dark, or silence, or weird night sounds, but back when Ana was alive, she'd pretend to be afraid of thunder just so she could pad down the hall to her big sister's room. Ana had this habit of going to bed early, like at nine at night, but then she'd wake up a couple hours later and stay up until three or four in the morning. She once told Jessica she liked feeling that she had not just the whole house but the whole neighborhood to herself.

When Jessica had gone to Ana's room during thunderstorms, Ana would usually be awake, wearing just her white underwear and a ratty old shirt. She'd be on her phone or painting her nails, sometimes both. She'd glance up from whatever it was she was doing, and even if Jessica was interrupting, she wouldn't act put out. She'd ask if Jessica was scared because of the thunder and if she wanted to hang out for a little while. Jessica would nod. Her little girl's heart would be beating so, so fast.

Usually, Jessica would pretend to fall asleep on Ana's floor, just so she could stay in the room longer and listen to her sister do all the things she did. Ana would experiment with eyeliner, put on face masks, and flip through weeks-old magazines. Sometimes she'd go into the bathroom, open the window, and turn on the vent. Jessica would open her eyes just enough to watch her sister pull out a cigarette and a matchbox from behind a stack of mismatched towels in the cabinet. Ana would sit there on the edge of the sink, wearing hardly anything, staring into the night, blowing clouds of smoke out the window. The girls' grandpa smoked, and the bitter smell always lingered on his breath, his hair, his hands, his clothes. Ana, though, always somehow smelled like her perfume, like linen.

John shouted Jessica's name. He was far away now. Jessica could hear some of the other people, too, shouting and laughing up in the choir loft. Someone screamed, scared by something or nothing. Someone else laughed. John shouted Jessica's name *again*. Then he barked it out, like he was angry, like he was through, like he didn't want to play this stupid game anymore.

Jessica's phone buzzed. She reached in her pocket to turn it off completely, and then continued to lie there, barefoot and with her ankles crossed. She interlaced her fingers on top of her stomach, listening.

She'd nearly fallen asleep when she heard the door to the cathedral open and footsteps come up the aisle. When she opened her eyes, she saw Peter Rojas's scuffed-up off-white sneakers approach and then come to a stop. Then Peter sat on the pew, right above Jessica.

"What are you doing?" Jessica whispered.

"I found you," Peter said. "I'm supposed to hide with you."

"Shouldn't you be at work?"

"I called in sick tonight."

Jessica clucked, mildly impressed that Peter had it in him to lie about anything. "You called in sick for *this*?"

Peter didn't reply, just shifted in his seat. Jessica waited. Peter didn't move.

"Go away," Jessica said. "Please."

"I don't think that's how this game works."

Jessica returned her gaze to the coin-sized wad of gum above her face, and when it was clear that Peter really wasn't leaving, she sighed.

"So," she asked. "Do you still sing?"

"No." Peter laughed. It sounded nice, had rhythm, like a stone skipping across water. "Not really."

"Why not?" Jessica asked. She couldn't help herself. "You used to be really good at it."

She was teasing, but she wasn't lying. Peter had been in the show choir, a group that went to nursing homes and

Jewish community centers to sing pop standards and show tunes for old people. Jessica knew that Peter's friends gave him unending amounts of shit for it, but he never seemed to care.

"That's kind of a long story," Peter replied.

The wooden pew squeaked as Peter again shifted his weight, and if she'd been a kind person, or even a normal person, she would've asked to hear the long story. It's not as if, in that moment, either of them had anything else to do, and Jessica found herself genuinely curious. If someone had enough musical talent to make people listen and clap along, what would it take to stop? That was a good question, but it never made it even close to the tip of her tongue. The question buried itself deeper and deeper inside her, the words more and more unsaid and unshared. Seconds ticked by, and pipes continued to bang somewhere in the depths of the church. The silence stretched out, but it wasn't awkward because Jessica didn't believe that any silence was awkward.

However many minutes later, the cathedral doors opened.

"Game's over," Peter said quietly.

Voices exploded into the cathedral, ricocheting off the stone, so loud and wrong-sounding that Jessica winced. She scooted out from under the pew but stayed sitting on the tile floor.

"Holy fuck!" Jenny cried out when she saw Jessica. "There you are. We were seriously about to leave without you."

Everyone was there, including John. Jessica gave him a bland smile.

Peter stood. "I just found her. Just like, a minute ago."

"Well, good." Jenny threw up her hands. "Game over. Let's get the hell out of here."

John asked Jenny to wait while he walked Jessica to her door. During the ride back, John had said nothing about how Jessica had ignored him in the church when his feet had been inches from her face. Instead, he'd just sat in the back seat of the Buick, with his arm slung across Jessica's shoulders, and shot the shit with Jenny. Was her brother still dating that girl? Did he like his new job? That's cool. That's cool.

It wasn't until Jessica was reaching for her keys that John finally spoke.

"Were you thanking Peter Rojas for saving you the other day?"

Jessica froze, her fingers grazing the door knob. "I . . . What?"

"Do you think I'm stupid?" John leaned in. Jessica felt the heat of his breath, oily and unwanted. "Did you think I wouldn't find out about that?"

"There's nothing to find out about," Jessica replied. "My car needed a jump, and he helped me out."

"You should've told me."

Jessica was all of a sudden very, very tired. It was late, and she thought that maybe the lack of sleep was making her hallucinate. There were fireflies in the yard. They flashed and dimmed, flashed and dimmed—in a rhythm, in time with one another. Like a song.

"You shouldn't hide things from me," John added.

Jessica was so worn out she thought maybe John was right. She could stand to be more open. It would hurt: to crack open her chest and pour out what little was there. But she was feeling bold, deliriously optimistic.

Jessica spun around. "Have you ever heard me sing?"

She went on before John could interrupt: "Before my sister died, I used to sing. I was in choir and pageants and stuff. I was really good. My teachers would tell me I was a natural."

Jessica mustered a smile, and in that bizarre, hopeful moment, she believed in the impossible. John had never heard her sing, not really. The only times he would've had the chance were in the car, along with the radio, or if she was listening to something on her headphones and thought she was alone.

John had glitter-gold eyes. He was beautiful when he wanted to be. A couple of nights ago, she'd asked him to fly away with her. It wasn't too, too hard to imagine them together in their little studio apartment. They wouldn't have furniture, but they would have each other. He would listen to her sing.

John said nothing, and Jessica realized he didn't know how to answer. She'd made a mistake. She'd wanted to give him a sliver of something rare and good about herself, and, instead, she'd backed him into a corner. She wanted her rare goodness to be a gift, but her timing was all fucked up.

Jessica knew her timing was all fucked up because John finally replied by asking, "Are you making fun of me?"

"What?" Jessica balked. "No. *No.*"

"John!" Jenny called out from the idling Buick. "John. Let's go!"

John held up his hand, silently commanding Jenny to wait. His gaze remained pinned on Jessica.

"Did you think I wouldn't find out about what happened with the car?" he asked, steering the conversation back. "With Peter?"

"Nothing *happened* with Peter," Jessica insisted. "You know I wouldn't do that to you. My battery was dead, and I needed help."

Help. The word tasted like shame, bitter like ash ground between her molars. She looked across the street at Hector's. Peter's truck wasn't there. There were no lights in the upstairs window. In her yard, the fireflies had stopped flashing.

John reached out and grabbed Jessica's wrist. He knew how to do it so it looked like a gesture of affection. He pressed his long fingers into her pulse point, then past it to where the tendons scraped against the bone.

Jessica winced, grinding her teeth. She didn't want to give in. She didn't need to apologize for this. She hadn't done anything wrong.

John pressed harder.

"I'm sorry," Jessica gasped. "I didn't tell you because I knew you'd be mad. It was a mistake. I'm sorry." She glanced over her shoulder toward the Buick, but Jenny was looking down, focused on her phone. Then she glanced to the house, to her upstairs window. Something—a fuzzy flicker of darkness behind the curtain—had caught her eye. It was barely there, then gone.

"Please," Jessica said. "I'm sorry, and I'm very tired."

John released his fingers, and then brought Jessica's wrist up to his lips. This was what mothers did: kiss away the hurt. He was disgusting. Jessica was ashamed that she'd ever wanted to give anything of herself to him. Her nails were so close to his face. She could tear across his skin, into his eye.

"I'll see you tomorrow."

John made his way across the yard and climbed into Jenny's car. Jessica could still feel the slickness of his saliva on her wrist. It felt like a violation, like she could wash and wash and the spit would always be there.

• • •

Minutes later, Jessica was standing in the rising steam of her shower, letting the water run through her hair. Out of the corner of her eye, she saw a shadow pass on the other side of the clear plastic curtain. Assuming it was just Iridian coming in to borrow a shirt or something, Jessica closed her eyes and dipped her head back. She liked to run the water as hot as possible for as long as she could, liked the challenge of standing beneath it until the feeling on her skin went from scalding to soothing. She'd started humming another old song from the pharmacy's playlist when she got the sense that something was . . . off. Her voice wasn't echoing in the same way. It felt like the space—the shower, the entire bathroom—had gotten smaller.

Jessica opened her eyes, and there, in front of her face, through the veil of steam and on the other side of the curtain, was a hand. Its dark palm was facing her. Its fingers were spread. The hand was so clear, Jessica could see the blurry swoop of a lifeline and the horizontal slashes on skin that marked the division between each individual finger bone. The hand pressed inward against the plastic, stretching it tight. Jessica jolted back, nearly losing her balance against the slick surface of the tub. She caught herself by smacking a wet hand against the tile. Then she did the only thing she could think to do: She stared straight at the hand and pushed her own hand against it. It was solid and fleshy. Jessica let out a garbled cry, then ripped back the shower curtain. There was no one. Nothing there.

Dripping wet and gulping down desperate breaths, Jessica grabbed a towel, ran into her bedroom, and then dashed down the hall to her sisters' room. Iridian was asleep in her bed. Jessica started to call out Rosa's name, but then clapped a hand over her mouth and collapsed back against the wall.

"Shit," she mumbled. "Holy *shit*."

She gripped the towel tighter around her chest.

"You're fine," she told herself. "Everything's fine."

Jessica found her balance on two shaky legs and went back into her bedroom, leaving behind her a trail of wet footprints. In the bathroom, she turned off the water in the shower, dried herself off completely, changed into a fresh pair of underwear and a shirt to sleep in, and started brushing out her long hair. It was all normal. Totally normal. The bristles of her brush caught on a knot. Jessica yanked and yanked, bringing tears to her eyes and snapping the strands from her scalp. She tried humming to herself again, but it was nothing, just a bunch of nonsense notes.

"You're fine," she told her reflection. "Everything's fine."

She braved a look back at the shower curtain, and saw, there in the condensation, the outline of a hand, perfectly centered, with beads of moisture dripping from its edges.

She dove toward the toilet and threw up.

Rosa

(Wednesday, June 12th)

ON WEDNESDAY MORNING, Rosa decided to search for the hyena in shifts. She left the house early and was heading back in the middle of the day to use the bathroom and refill her thermos when she felt the shift in the wind.

The day had been bright and hot and humid, but then, all of a sudden, it wasn't. The entire eastern sky was dark, the color of pigeon feathers. That dark sky pushed a wall of cool wind right into Rosa, blowing back her unbound hair and the fabric of her long dress, blowing back the leaves on the trees. Rain was coming.

Rosa took off into a jog, ignoring how the jolting movement caused the stiff leather of her shoes to scrape against her heels. The thermos in her backpack bounced hard against her spine. The pigeon-colored sky was now all around. The wind was blowing so hard that loose leaves and bits of trash were tumbling down the street. A cup from a fast-food restaurant skittered and spun on the asphalt. The dogs in the neighborhood—both inside houses and out in yards—took up yipping and howling. The rain started to fall, leaving circles the size of checkers on the concrete sidewalk. The drops were so big, they felt like pennies when they hit the top of Rosa's head.

When Rosa rounded the corner, she saw Jessica's car a little ways down, parked in front of their house. Wednesdays were her days off from the pharmacy. Despite the rain, Jessica's arm was hanging out her driver's-side window, and her middle finger was tapping against the door.

Rosa got closer, approaching the car from the back. There was a jolt of movement, and it took her a split second to process what she'd seen: John had reached over and taken hold of Jessica by the neck. Jessica's hand, the one that was extended out the window, tensed and then smacked the outside of her car door. Jessica's head jerked to the side, like she was trying to pull it away.

Rosa gasped, froze briefly, and then started running. When she reached the car, she could see John gripping Jessica's chin. Her sister's neck looked painfully twisted, and she shouted something—*stop* or *off*—at which point Rosa whacked her palm against the closed passenger-side window. John immediately released Jessica and spun around.

"What's going on?" Rosa demanded through the glass.

"Nothing." John's voice was muffled. "We were just talking."

"Yeah." Rosa glanced at her sister, who was staring straight through the windshield, her jaw clenched. "Looks like it."

John opened his door so quickly that Rosa nearly tripped over her own feet as she backed away.

"I'm walking home," he said. "See you later, Jess. Later, Rosa."

Neither sister responded. Rosa watched John make his way down the sidewalk, slouched forward against the rain and with his hands in his pockets. She looked at the street, then over to Hector's house. The front door was open, and just the storm door was closed. A single lamp was glowing in the depths of the darkened living room. She looked up to the second-floor window and what she knew was Hector Garcia's room. A light was on in there, too. A shadow passed behind the curtain. Hector and his friends were there, watching. They thought they were protectors, which was a silly thing all boys thought.

Jessica kept sitting in her car, staring through the rain-blurred windshield. Only after John had turned down a side street a block away did she finally get out and head toward the house. She passed right by Rosa as if she wasn't there.

"I don't like him," Rosa called after her. "Has he done this before? Why haven't you told any—"

"Don't start," Jessica snapped. "He's just in a bad mood."

"He's *always* in a bad mood, Jessie."

They stopped together at the front door, under the shelter of the awning. Rosa could see the pink marks on Jessica's skin from where John's fingertips had dug in. This wasn't the first time Rosa had told her sister how she felt about John, and it wasn't the first time Jessica had gotten defensive about it. If Rosa pushed, Jessica would tell her that she had *no idea* what it was like to be in a relationship, that Rosa shouldn't *dare* act like she knew what went on between a girl and a guy in love because Rosa hadn't even been kissed yet or had anyone touch her. That last part, about the kissing and the touching, wasn't true, but Rosa never said anything about it. She had the right to her own secrets.

Still, though. This was different. Rosa had always known that John was mean and that Jessica always jumped when he said jump, but this was the first time she'd seen evidence of him touching her sister in an aggressive way. Had there been signs? Had she missed them?

"Don't tell Dad," Jessica said, as she unlocked the front door.

"Alright." Rosa's heart broke a little. "Of course. If that's what you want."

"I've been telling him I want to leave," Jessica said. "That's why he's in a bad mood."

"Leave *him*?" Rosa asked, startled. "Like, break up with him?"

"No." Jessica paused. "Like, leave San Antonio."

"Oh." Rosa shook a drop of rain from the tip of her nose. "Where would you go?"

Jessica shrugged. She looked tired. Her mascara was flaking off. There were little specks of black around her eyes, and her lipstick was smudged. There was a blur of dark red on her jaw, from where John had pulled the color away from her mouth.

"Austin, maybe? Maybe the Valley to stay with Aunt Francine. Anywhere but here. I asked him to come with me, but he doesn't want to."

"You should go by yourself," Rosa told Jessica. "If that's what you want to do."

"It's not that easy." Jessica pulled her key from the door and faltered, like that little flick of her wrist had exhausted her completely. "You wouldn't understand."

Jessica turned, and Rosa wondered if her sister's weary appearance was due to something more than what had just happened with John. It seemed like an older weariness, like one that had tidily tucked itself inside her. Rosa didn't ask *Are you okay?* or *Did something happen?* because it was clear that something *had* happened and Jessica was *not* okay.

"Do you think . . . ?" Jessica crinkled her nose, like she did when she was uncomfortable but didn't want anyone to know she was uncomfortable. "Do you think there's something wrong with the house?"

Rosa didn't know how to respond. All sorts of things were wrong with the house. Pick a room, pick a cabinet in a room. Open the door, and there were reminders of dead women. Look at the floor, look at the wall. There were scuffs and scratches of lives lived. Was it possible for a house to be abandoned and still have four people living in it?

"What do you mean?" Rosa asked.

Jessica's teeth dragged across her bottom lip, pulling the color off even more. There *was* something wrong, something really wrong.

"Nothing," Jessica replied. She opened the door. "Forget I said anything."

Rosa knew it was a lie, but what could she do? It was impossible to force the rain to stop falling. It was just as impossible to force the truth out of her sister when she was determined to keep it locked up tight.

Rosa was a searcher, though. She was determined and had ways of finding things.

Iridian

(Wednesday, June 12th)

IRIDIAN'S NOTEBOOK WAS down at her feet, open and with the pages spread wide. She must've kicked it there while she'd been napping. She fumbled in her blankets, trying to find her pen, but it wouldn't have been the first time one of them had been lost for days in the folds of fabric or wedged tight in the space between her bed and the wall.

It was raining outside, pretty hard from the sound of it. Iridian could hear the whoosh of wind and the drums of drops against the windows and the roof. It wasn't night, just the middle of the afternoon according to the clock on her nightstand, but her entire room was in shades of gray. It was dreary and wonderful. She would've stayed in bed for hours more if she hadn't needed a glass of water.

Iridian stepped into the hall and then stopped. The hall, the house—everything—smelled like oranges. The air conditioner clicked on and blew out orange-scented air. She closed her eyes and could picture herself back at Francine's place in South Texas, out in the dry air and the orange trees. She took another step and yelped as the bare sole of her right foot landed on something hard and thin. She looked down, and there it was: her pen. It must've gotten caught up in her waistband and then fallen out as she walked from her room. As she bent to pick it up, a mark on the wall—scrawled there in blue ink on the white paint, just an inch or so from the baseboard—caught her eye. It started off as a series of broken lines—light tick marks— but then those marks started to merge with curves and loops. The loops turned into letters. The letters formed words. The ink became darker, the lines thicker, as if the hand holding the pen had become more sure of itself.

I want him   I want him to want me

A hard breath burst from Iridian's lungs.

"Ana," she whispered.

Those words were Iridian's words—from the story she'd just been working on. The writing, though— especially the letter *a*'s, handwritten in the typed-out style, with the little umbrella-curl on top—was Ana's, without a doubt.

Iridian didn't know how long she waited for her sisters to come home—minutes? an hour? She also didn't really remember going downstairs. Mostly she remembered sitting on the couch, her spine too straight, and being haunted by the smell of oranges—so strong it was making her sick.

When her sisters did come home, Rosa rushed to Iridian's side. The fabric of her dress was soggy from the rain, and Iridian gripped it tight, squeezing out water. Jessica stood by the end of the couch. Her hair was in a ponytail, but it didn't look right. It was lopsided, puffed, like she'd been running through the woods and branches had snagged her long locks. A dark splotch the size and shape of a peanut shell stood out on her cheek.

"My words," Iridian told her sisters. "Ana's writing. Upstairs."

"I'll go look," Rosa said.

While Rosa was upstairs, Jessica just stood there, doing nothing and saying nothing. Iridian gazed at the blank television screen. She tried to swallow, but it felt like her tongue was a wad of cotton.

"I saw her hand," Jessica eventually said.

"It smells like oranges," Iridian said. "Do you smell it?"

There was a pause. "No," Jessica replied.

"Why is she doing this?" Iridian asked.

Jessica didn't respond.

After a while, Rosa came back downstairs.

"I taped up a piece of paper," she said. "You can't see it anymore."

That was a fine fix, but Iridian knew it would be a long time before she went upstairs again. She was under attack, and the only thing she knew to do was hide.

The First Time Ana Torres
Came Back as a Ghost

SOME NIGHTS, BEFORE Ana would undress at her bedroom window, she'd go out into the street. Wearing white Keds, a long T-shirt, and short shorts, Ana would march under the light of the street lamps. She was practicing to be a majorette, which was something we'd heard her mom had done back when she was in high school.

We'd watch Ana hurl a silver baton into the dark sky, and then spin around with her gaze up. Over and over. Ana could spin. She had that down. She could march. She could toss her baton so high it nearly grazed the telephone wires, but the problem was, she could hardly ever catch it once it came back down. Something about her aim was bad. Her fingers always grasped but never caught. The baton would ricochet off her hand, bounce against the asphalt, and skitter away. Ana never gave up, though. Again and again, she'd snatch up the baton and head right back into the middle of the street. Once there, she'd tick up her chin, press one fist against her waist, cock out her elbow, and prepare to lead the vast, invisible band behind her.

We were the first people to witness Ana come back as a ghost, and we considered ourselves lucky. She died in June, and we saw her again in August. It happened at night, when hauntings typically happen. We were in Hector's room. It was late, way past midnight, when we heard thumps at the window—not like rocks being thrown because that sounds like *ping, ping*—but actual *thumps*, like the soft knocking a knuckle makes on wood. This was particularly weird because Hector's bedroom was upstairs.

Calvin was closest to the window. He crawled up on his hands and knees and slowly pulled the curtains back. There was no one on the other side, of course, just the night sky and the light coming in from the street lamps. He looked over his shoulder and laughed.

"You're all such pussies," he said.

Just as he was about to release the curtain, Calvin turned back to the window, this time looking out and down, toward the street. His expression spun from humor to horror, and for a moment he was frozen. He made a choking sound and then fell backward.

Jimmy vaulted over Calvin to get to the window. He yanked the curtain back and also froze, just for a second, but then his face broke out into a smile. His eyes grew wide; they started to glisten. He reached out and put his palm on the glass pane, gently.

Deep down, we all knew the one thing—the one *person*—that could make Jimmy's face light up with that amount of joy and awe. We flew from our scattered places around the room, pulled a pale and still-stammering Calvin up from the floor, and huddled behind Jimmy. We looked out the window and down.

It was Ana. Of course it was Ana.

All things appear ghostly under the weak light of street lamps, and so that was how Ana appeared. We knew it was her because she was standing with her back to us. How many times had we seen that back, the swoops of those shoulders and hips? Even though the ghost of Ana Torres was wearing an oversized white T-shirt that came down to mid-thigh, we knew that body beneath. It was seared into our minds. Ana wasn't in her room, though, and she wasn't undressing. She wasn't in the street with her baton, either. Instead, she was in her front yard. Her pose, in a way, mirrored Jimmy's. She was facing the window of her dad's first-floor bedroom, with her hand up, but instead of pressing her palm flat to the glass, she was knocking against it with her knuckle.

The ghost of Ana Torres continued her steady knocking, and up in Hector's room, we could hardly breathe.

Eventually, the porch light at the Torres house flicked on. Ana's ghost turned its head slowly toward it. The front door opened, then the screen door, and then out came Rafe. We pushed back from the window and closed the curtain, leaving just an inch-wide gap for us all to peer through.

"Who's that?" Rafe shouted into the night. He was shirtless, wearing baggy jean shorts and holding a baseball bat. He took a couple of steps out into the yard, heading in the direction of the window.

Ana, though, was gone. We don't know how it happened. We never saw her fade out, evaporate, twitch like static and then disappear. She was just . . . gone. There, then not.

We watched Rafe stalk around the yard for a bit, calling out, making threats into the quiet night while smacking the bat into his open palm. He finally went inside, but the porch light stayed on. We drew back the curtains again and waited, staying up until dawn, hoping beyond hope that Ana would come back, but she never did.

It was Hector who finally broke the silence: "So what do we do now?"

Watching Ana undress and watching Ana twirl her

baton were our secrets to keep. But this—this felt too big and too *not ours* not to share with the Torres girls.

"We should leave Rosa a note," Jimmy said. "In her tree."

So that's what we did.

Several years ago, Rafe had tied a thick rope to one of the larger branches of the old oak tree in the front yard, and then fixed a knot at the bottom of the rope to serve as a foothold. It was a swing. Rosa was the only one who ever used it. She'd be out there for hours, pumping her knees to take herself higher. She'd cry out with joy, content with entertaining herself.

There was also a hollow in that tree. It faced away from the street, and we used to watch Rosa store things in that hollow—little things she'd find in the neighborhood like feathers or small stones or shards of colored glass. That hollow was the best place we could think to leave the note. The mailbox was out of the question. Did any of the girls have a cell phone? We had no idea, and if they did, none of us knew any of their numbers.

It took us most of the morning to get our message just right. We wanted it to be short and to say the right thing and to not have any major misspellings.

Calvin had the best handwriting, so he wrote it, in blue ballpoint pen on paper torn from a composition book. Hector volunteered to run over and put it in the tree.

We never saw Rosa retrieve the note, but a couple of days later, Hector's mom called us from downstairs saying that a letter had been left in the mailbox addressed to "Hector & His Friends." We ran downstairs, took the letter into the backyard, and crowded around as Hector unfolded it.

Rosa's writing, in pencil on heart-shaped stationery, was so light. When the sun hit the paper, the words were nearly invisible.

Thank you for telling me about my sister, she'd written. *I hope she comes back. If she doesn't, I will go out and try to find her myself.*

Rosa
(Wednesday, June 12th)

ROSA HAD TO wait almost an hour before she could speak with Father Mendoza, so once she took her seat in front of his wide oak desk, she placed her hands into her lap, leaned forward, and got right to the meat of the thing.

"Good afternoon, Father," she said. "I'd like to know what Catholic doctrine has to say about ghosts."

Father Mendoza was a tall, thin man originally from the Rio Grande Valley. Rosa thought he looked like he was made of sticks, and he always smelled somewhat brittle, like dry kindling about to catch fire. It was true that, shortly after arriving at San Fernando, Father Mendoza, in his attempt to counsel Rafe when they'd come across each other in the grocery store, had gotten punched in the face. Father Mendoza had then promised Rafe he'd leave the Torres family alone, but Rosa wouldn't have any of that. Nearly every week since Ana had died, Rosa had sat right there—at that oak desk, with her hands folded in her lap—and asked her priest questions about faith and kindness and doubt and death. The marks Ana had left on the wall hadn't scared Rosa, hadn't made her wild-eyed and twitchy like they'd made Iridian or pale and mute like they'd made Jessica. When she'd first seen them, and traced the blue ink lightly with the tips of her fingers, she'd smiled. Her heart had bloomed like the big white petals on the magnolia trees in the park. With one beat, it had tripled in size. Her sister had come back. Within seconds, though, that smile faded. Ana's marks on the wall were so broken, and the lines were so wobbly. Ana may have been back, but something was wrong. If the lines were broken and wobbly, then Ana's spirit was broken and wobbly, too. Rosa was worried.

"Well." Father Mendoza put his hands in his lap and leaned forward in his chair just as Rosa had done. "Unfortunately, church doctrine isn't completely clear. There's a lot on demons, but less on ghosts. Basically, we view them as souls lost in purgatory, stuck between heaven and hell because they need to make amends or atone for something. Some of them are harmless wanderers. Others are angry and play tricks." The priest sat quietly for a moment. "Why do you ask?"

Play tricks, Rosa repeated to herself. And then she said, out loud, "I think my sister Ana has come back."

Father Mendoza didn't smirk or snicker, which Rosa appreciated.

"Have you seen her?" he asked.

"No," Rosa replied. "But others have. And she's doing things."

Rosa looked away from Father Mendoza's light brown eyes and stared off into the corner of the room, thinking. She liked this room. She liked the walls, which were painted stark white—white like the blossoms on a magnolia tree. She liked the fact that nothing hung on the stark white walls except for a cross and a small ticking clock. The room was always clean. She could do a lot of good thinking in a room like this. The only thing that broke the perfection of the clean, white room was the row of sugar ants marching up the wall behind Father Mendoza's chair.

Ants sought shelter indoors during the rain, when their home in the ground outside got too wet. That made sense. Living creatures want to be comfortable, dry, and safe in familiar territory. If Ana was a spirit trapped in purgatory, she must've been very uncomfortable.

"I can tell you this," Father Mendoza went on. "If God has willed Ana's spirit to return, and if God has willed you and your family to bear witness, you must be accepting and receptive to her and whatever that message might be."

Father Mendoza then cleared his throat and glanced up at his clock. Rosa knew there were other people out in the hall who had come after her and were waiting to speak to the priest, but still, she'd been in his office for barely ten minutes.

"Do you have any idea what your sister's message might be?" the priest asked.

"Not yet," Rosa replied. "But I'll figure it out."

On her way out of the church, she came across Walter Mata blocking one of the hallways. He was up on a ladder, changing a light that had burned out. The sight of him caused Rosa to stop short. Her breath came out in a single, strange pop. She knew that, in addition to being both a grade ahead of her in school and her ride to church every Sunday, Walter worked at the church a few days a week, doing odd jobs. He'd fix leaky toilets, change air filters, sweep, mop, empty trashcans, whatever anyone needed him to do. In order to change the light, Walter's right hand was raised toward the ceiling, and the muscles in his arm were twitching as he screwed in the new bulb. Rosa liked the look of that arm. She thought, *Huh*.

"Hey," Walter said, noticing Rosa.

"Hi," Rosa replied. Then she scooted past the ladder legs and went on her way. There were other things to think about right then aside from the unexpected shock-delight of Walter Mata with his arm raised, changing a light.

• • •

Rosa's own room wasn't a very good place for thinking. It wasn't wide open like the yard or good and clean like Father Mendoza's office. Her room was a mess, but she'd never dream of going into Jessica's room, which was an even bigger mess and where she wasn't sure she'd be able to find a cleared-off space to sit.

So, for a while, Rosa sat on the floor of her mess of a bedroom. She sat and waited. She listened. She sniffed at the musty air, hoping to pick up on Ana's cottony scent. She sat through several cycles of the air conditioner clicking off and on. Downstairs, she heard voices coming from the television. Iridian was down there. She was on the couch, burrowed under a blanket and watching soap operas. The volume on the television was turned almost all the way down. The voices of the characters were just murmurs rising up through the floor, but the sound of them still tugged on Rosa's nerves.

She relented, and went down the hall to Jessica's room, but just to pass through to get to the window, and then to the oak tree outside the window. After shoving up the sash and sticking her head into the humid night, Rosa saw a spot on the trunk of the tree, a fresh blond oval that stood out against the darker strips of bark. It was a scar. A year later and the tree was still healing from the night when Ana had put her trust in a branch that couldn't hold her weight. Rosa could relate to the tree. She knew what it felt like to have a part of her snapped off, leaving her with a big, raw hole that might heal but would never heal right.

Rosa was careful with her footing. The recent rains had made the bark soft and slick. First she climbed out, and then she climbed up, hooking a leg over a branch above, pulling and twisting until she was on top of that branch, belly down. She shimmied forward, knocking loose leaves and small branches, until she could latch on to the gutter in front of her and pull herself onto the roof. She'd only gone up to the roof a few times before, and every time she'd ended up with oak leaves in her hair and scrapes along her forearms from pulling herself along the gritty tiles. It was always a fight.

Rosa much preferred being on the ground to being in the sky. She liked having a connection to the earth, and was comforted by the thought of miles and miles of life beneath her feet. But the sky reminded Rosa of her sister: Ana, who wanted to fly away from Southtown. Ana, who seemed to always stand on the tips of her toes as if she *could* fly away from Southtown.

From up on the roof, Rosa couldn't hear the television, but of course there were other sounds. There were shouts from backyards, from kids playing before dinnertime. Garage doors opened and closed. A couple of streets away, a construction crew was finishing up for the day, and she could hear the last few rapid-fire punches of nails from their guns. Above Rosa's head came the roar of airplanes, taking off from or coming in to the nearby airport.

Rosa had just found a place to sit near the peak of the roof when she heard a rustle from the oak tree. The leaves then shook, but it was too small a shake to have been caused by a squirrel. Rosa took a step back down toward the tree. It was dim in the twilight, but she swore she could see dark red deep in the tree. Her first thought was that it was the wing of a lonely bird.

Rosa took another step and lost her balance. There was no traction between the sole of one of her shoes and the roof tile, so her right foot slid forward six inches. She fell on her left knee and caught herself in an awkward split. Rosa closed her eyes and let out a breath. Another airplane flew overhead. When she opened her eyes she saw the red again, deep in the leaves. Crouching, Rosa leaned forward as far as she could. She didn't look down.

"I'm here, I'm here," Rosa said, pressing the palms of her hands into the roof tiles to gain as much traction as possible. She wanted to be ready for anything. Then she said, "Play tricks."

Iridian

(Friday, June 14th)

THERE WAS NOTHING like standing in the middle of the orange groves in the summer in South Texas. The scent hung so heavy it wasn't even necessary to really breathe it in. It was there, always—that oily bite, that sting of citrus.

Iridian had only stood in the middle of the orange groves—the ones down in Mission that belonged to her aunt Francine—at two points in her life. The first time was when she was just over a year old and had walked without having to hold her mother's hand. Of course she didn't remember that. The second time was three years ago, the summer when she was thirteen, when Francine had come up to San Antonio to take Iridian and her sisters for a long weekend over the summer. There had been four of them.

Ana had been alive then. The long weekend had turned into a week had turned into a week and a half.

Iridian remembered the smell of oranges most of all, but also the feel of the wind, in particular how that wind would blow dust that would then get caught in her hair—all the way from her scalp to the ends. She'd liked the gritty feel, and would go days without taking a shower.

Iridian also remembered the day Rafe came. There was no wind that day. The girls had just finished breakfast when they heard his truck approaching, rattling like a sick person. While Iridian and her sisters had stayed seated at the table, Francine went to meet Rafe at the door. There had been shouting. Iridian had plucked out a few of Rafe's words: *kidnapped, mine, no right.* Ana had looked to her sisters and then had taken a bite of buttered toast.

"Don't worry," she'd told them, smacking crumbs from her lips. "We'll come back."

"We'd better," Iridian had said.

In the truck, on the way back to San Antonio, crammed between Rosa and Jessica, Iridian chewed on the end of her braid, sucking up the dust and the bitter smell of oranges.

She wasn't a writer then, or even that obsessive a reader, so she didn't yet know the pure joy that came along with smelling the pages of books, how a new book smelled like chlorine or how a used book sometimes smelled like cigarettes or tangy breath. All she loved that summer was being coated in dust and the smell of oranges.

And now, it made Iridian mad thinking about how much she once loved being outside. It made her particularly mad on a night like this one, when she was on the couch in the living room, covered up by a crocheted blanket and pretending to be asleep. She had been clamping her jaw shut for so long that a headache had taken root and bloomed behind her right eye. She was angry, but she was also scared—angry at herself for being so scared. She couldn't help it. The house had been making sounds all night. Windowpanes in the kitchen were shifting in their sashes. The refrigerator kept clicking. Ice cubes were falling from the door to the floor and shattering, one every half hour or so. The sounds then got closer. The ceiling fan above her head creaked. Something—a fly maybe—buzzed around her head, but then it stayed in one place, and the buzzing got louder and more persistent. Maybe she was making that up. Maybe it was just a symptom of her headache.

Then, Iridian heard the click and fizz of a soda can being opened. She tossed the blanket aside and sat up, knowing exactly what she was going to see: Jessica holding a Diet Coke. She didn't have any makeup on—not even the faintest flick of mascara—and she was wearing red plaid pajama bottoms and a blue-striped tank top. Her socks didn't match. There was a ragged hole in one, at the big toe. It was jarring—the clashing patterns, the bare face. Iridian hadn't seen Jessica look so un-put-together in a long time.

"Hey," Jessica said. "Do you know where Dad is?"

"What are you lurking around for?" Iridian demanded. "What time is it, anyway?"

"After three." Jessica slurped her soda. "Dad should be home by now."

"Why don't you just call him?" Iridian asked.

"He's not answering his phone."

Didn't they just have this conversation?

Iridian waited, then waited some more, but Jessica just kept standing there. Finally, Iridian rolled onto her side, burrowing her face into the cushions of the couch.

"You can't stay down here forever, you know," Jessica said.

"I can try!" Iridian shouted.

If she closed her eyes and thought about it really, really hard, she could feel the fibers of the cheap, scratchy couch and those of the cheap, scratchy crocheted blanket weaving together with the hairs of her arms and unshaved legs. Those fibers poked into the skin of Iridian's face, trapping her there, pincushion-style. She would become the furniture. The furniture would become her.

Iridian had been downstairs for two days now, camped out on the couch. This was her haunted life. She slept whenever—it didn't necessarily have to be night. When the seemingly never-ending storms weren't causing the power to blink out, she'd watch the channel on satellite that showed only soap operas, one episode after the other after the other. She was vaguely aware of her dad and her sisters coming and going, passing behind the couch on their way to and from the front door and the kitchen. Jessica was going to work or to John's. Rosa was going to church or to look for her hyena. Rafe was maybe going to work, maybe going to the bar, maybe going to sad Norma Galván's house a couple of blocks away.

Iridian hadn't changed her clothes. She hadn't taken a shower. Eventually, Rosa had warmed Iridian a can of tomato soup and brought down a toothbrush and some toothpaste from upstairs.

Iridian mourned the absence of her books. She'd find herself reaching for them, involuntarily. She missed the feeling of paper against her fingers. The loss was painful. The pain wasn't in her heart, but in her throat, where words come from.

"I keep waiting for something else to happen," Iridian said. "Every little sound makes me want to jump out of my skin." She paused. "Have you seen anything?"

"What are you watching?" Jessica asked, sitting on the edge of the couch. She yanked on the corner of the blanket to try to gather enough to cover her legs. "Anything good?"

"Go away." Iridian swatted at her sister's arm. "There's no room."

Jessica took another noisy slurp of soda, and the sound caused Iridian's headache to pulse.

"That lady has a weird mouth," she said, nodding toward the screen. "Seriously. These actors are so ugly. Where do they find these people?"

Jessica scooted her butt back, squashing Iridian's feet into the cracks between the cushions. "Get your giant-ass crane legs out of the way," she said. "You should write for soaps. You'd be good at that, right?"

"I . . ." Iridian hesitated. "Maybe?"

What was happening? Iridian stared at the side of her sister's face, which was lit up by the flashing screen. Who was this alternate, compliment-bearing version of Jessica? It wasn't the sneering version, the one who talked to Iridian as if she didn't have a brain in her head or a heart in her chest. It wasn't the hard and silent version, the one who wanted everyone to believe she was made up of wires and cold plates of metal, welded together tight.

This version of Jessica was just hanging out, sucking on a Diet Coke, seeming totally absorbed in a scene on low volume between a middle-aged woman wearing a slinky designer gown pointing a gun at another middle-aged woman wearing a slinky designer gown. Everything seemed so *normal*. Jessica hadn't said another thing about Ana or Ana's *hand* or the writing on the wall.

With her gaze still on the screen, Jessica pulled more of the blanket toward her, tucking it up and under her chin. Iridian was left with a corner that only covered her from the waist down. She was sort of cold now, but it actually wasn't that bad: two of the Torres sisters sitting together on the couch, watching soaps.

"This blanket smells," Jessica eventually said.

"*You* smell," Iridian replied.

Jessica cracked a smile, and Iridian ate it up.

Jessica

JESSICA HAD ONLY two memories of her mother, but they were both so old she didn't know if they were real or if she'd invented them. The first was simple. It was of her mother standing outside, backlit by the sun. Her bare legs were copper-brown, and there was a crease of sweat behind each of her knees. Her nails were short, round, and not polished. She was wearing three gold rings that Rafe had given her on three separate occasions, all stacked up on one finger. Aside from those rings and a small gold cross that hung around her neck, she wasn't wearing any other jewelry.

The second memory Jessica had of her mother was of them in the car together. Ana was also there. This memory Jessica was almost positive she'd made up, because she would've been only four years old and strapped in a car seat in the back when it had happened. Ana was in the front, even though Jessica knew now that her sister would have been too young to be riding shotgun. It was cold outside. Ana was wearing a puffy pink coat that was dirty around the wrists and had probably been bought secondhand. The heater wheezed. After easing through a stop sign, Jessica's mom reached over and took Ana's hand.

"Hold your breath," she'd commanded.

They'd been driving through a graveyard. It was on both sides of the car, as if the cemetery had been there first and the street had later been plowed through it. There were tall iron gates and tilted stones. Most of the writing on those stones had been rubbed smooth. Names and the dates of long or short lives had dissolved along with the bones below. The graves went on and on. Jessica's eyes were starting to water from holding her breath for so long.

Finally, after they'd driven through to the other side, Jessica's mom dropped Ana's hand and told both of her daughters a story. It was about how, when she was a girl, she went to her uncle's funeral. She didn't have a good coat, so she stood there shivering throughout the graveside service in a long-sleeved wool dress. Once she got home, she stood in front of the radiator until the sun went down, but she couldn't get warm. At dinner, she ate chicken soup that turned cold when it hit her tongue. After dinner, she took a hot bath, but she was still freezing. She put on a bunch of clothes, heaped blankets on her bed, and climbed into it. Still, she shivered. Nothing like this had ever happened to her before. She told her mother she thought she was sick. Her mother—the girls' grandmother—brought her hot licorice tea and told her that, no, she wasn't sick. She was just unlucky. Some of the dead people in the graveyard, her mother said, release mal aires, which enter a living person's body through the holes in their heads, like their nostrils and their mouths. It can happen any time of year, but especially in winter, when the ground is frozen and the corpses are uncomfortable.

"That's what happened," Rita Torres told her daughters.

During the funeral, mal aires had worked their way into her body. They wrapped around her bones and fastened themselves to her muscles. They dug in and gave her chills. They wanted her to know what it felt like to be dead. Rita's mother told her the feeling would pass in a day, and if it didn't, she'd take her to a lady who knew how to deal with these kinds of things.

The feeling didn't pass. It got worse. Jessica's mom woke up in the middle of the night with aches in her ears. By morning, one of her eardrums had burst. Fluid started leaking down the side of her neck. There was something in her head, pushing against skull bones, and it wanted something—it wanted to get out, or it wanted *her* to get out and make more room.

Jessica's grandmother drove her mother across town to some lady's house. That lady had just finished making ham sandwiches for her young sons when they'd arrived. She washed her hands and led her mom into a back bedroom. Once there, she rubbed alcohol on Rita's head, pressed her thumbs across her eyebrows, and whispered a short prayer. She told Rita to go home and take baths in hot salt water, twice a day.

The next morning, Rita was still a little chilly, but better. The day after that, she was back to normal.

Many years later, long after their mother had died, Ana asked Jessica if she remembered this story. Jessica said she did—she remembered sitting in the back seat, looking at Ana's dirty sleeves, and watching their mom reach over and grip her small hand.

"So you held your breath?" Ana asked. "That whole time?"

Jessica nodded. "I still do—every time I go past a graveyard. What about you?"

"I never even tried," Ana said, with a flash of a grin. "So who knows how many angry spirits I've been carrying around with me all this time."

Jessica

(Friday, June 14th)

"SIGN PETER'S CARD?"

Jessica looked up from her dinner of caramel corn and chocolate milk. Her manager, an older lady named Mathilda, was holding out a red envelope and a pen. Jessica was confused.

"What?"

Mathilda gave the envelope a little shake. "Peter's card. Everyone's signed it but you."

Jessica was still confused. "Is he sick?"

Peter didn't look sick. The last time she'd seen him was yesterday when they'd passed each other between shifts. She'd been in the employee bathroom for nearly half an hour, clipping her fingernails and then shaving her armpits over the sink. When she'd finally come out, there was Peter, leaning against the wall, waiting. He'd smiled and said hey, like it was no big deal that Jessica had hogged the bathroom for way too long. Even under the harsh fluorescent store light that made everything it touched look bleached and corpselike, he appeared easy, relaxed, like he was outside waiting for the bus on a warm spring day. Peter was infuriating.

"Are you kidding?" Mathilda asked, her smile crooked. "His last day is Sunday."

"Sunday?" Jessica replied. "As in, two days from now?"

"Well . . . yeah."

Jessica blew past Mathilda and charged out into the store. Her shift had been over for almost half an hour, so she'd changed out of her work shirt and into a gray V-neck that used to belong to John. She still had her khakis on, though, and the fabric swished when she walked. A Celine Dion ballad was blasting through the store speakers. It was the ironic soundtrack of her life.

Jessica found Peter in the candy aisle, up near the registers, where he was stuffing handful after handful of chocolate truffles into display boxes.

Peter heard the harsh swish of Jessica's khakis and glanced over his shoulder. Nope, he didn't look sick. He looked pretty great in that too-tall, easy-breezy way of his. If anything, Jessica was the one who looked sick. She'd stopped showering at home and was now practically living out of the store and out of her car. As a result, her hair and makeup had suffered. Jessica made excuses for herself—*to herself*—claiming the light was just too bad in the store's bathroom, but really she'd stopped caring.

"Oh, hey," Peter said.

"Mathilda told me you're leaving," Jessica blurted. "She asked me to sign your card."

"Oh. Nice. A card. Thanks for telling me."

"Where are you going?"

"College," Peter replied. "Up in San Marcos. But I'm going to visit family in Mexico for a couple weeks before that." He scooped up another handful of truffles. "What are you still doing here? I thought you'd be long gone by now."

"You didn't tell me that," Jessica snapped. "I didn't know that. About you leaving." She paused. "You're just a junior. You can't leave yet."

"I've been taking dual credit," Peter said. "Besides, I . . . didn't think you'd want to know."

Peter waited for Jessica to reply, which wasn't happening because Jessica didn't know how to reply. Did she really care about the details of her coworker's life? She had enough going on in her own life, in her *own house*. And, oh crap, Peter had that look on his face again, brows creased, mouth slightly puckered with concern, like he was about to ask Jessica how she was doing. She dreaded hearing that question—or some variation of that question—so much

that she started to shift up onto the balls of her feet, pre-
paring to turn and break into a sprint. Peter didn't ask
that question, though. He didn't say anything. Instead,
he plucked one of the chocolate truffles from the pile,
unwrapped it, and then popped it into his mouth. He
unwrapped another and held it out to Jessica.

Fast like a whip, Jessica snatched the chocolate from
Peter's fingers and tossed it in her mouth.

"Holy shit, you're a thief." Jessica chomped on the
chocolate as fast as she could to get rid of the evidence.
"Peter Rojas, I would've never expected. What would your
abuela in Mexico say if she knew?"

Peter licked the chocolate off his fingers. "I've never
done that before."

"Sure."

"You're a bad influence."

"The worst."

Jessica crouched down and took her keys from her
pocket, poised to dig into a strip of tape. "Do you need
help or anything?"

"Yeah, sure," Peter replied.

For nearly an hour, Jessica and Peter restocked almost
the entire candy aisle. Jessica opened boxes of peppermints
and cinnamon chews and those puffy things shaped like
peanuts. Occasionally, Peter left to help with the registers,
but, for the most part, they worked together, largely in
silence, which Jessica appreciated. She of course knew all

the words to all the songs that came through the speaker, but she didn't sing along. She caught herself humming once or twice but cut that off quick.

"Are you going to be at the block party tomorrow?" Peter eventually asked. He was across the aisle, with his back to Jessica, rearranging price tags.

Jessica paused, dropping a pack of Swedish Fish in her lap. She hadn't gone last year because the party had fallen on one of the days immediately following Ana's death. Or maybe the neighbors had canceled the party out of respect. She couldn't remember. That time was always a little fuzzy.

"I don't know," she said. "I work Saturday mornings. I could be there later. What about you?"

"You aren't picking up your phone."

Both Jessica and Peter turned at the sound of John's voice. That voice—Jessica had never thought much about it before, but now it grated. It felt itchy, itchy and cold like a ghost in her bones. Jessica realized she was wearing John's T-shirt, and she was tempted to strip it from her skin. She plucked at the fabric, shook her shoulders a little bit.

John had already apologized for what had happened the other day in the car, bought Jessica some roses—wilted pink ones from the grocery store—and took her out for soft serve. He'd do better, he'd said. Jessica had forgiven him but not really. She'd said the words *it's okay*, but she hadn't meant them. Every day in the work bathroom, she inspected the little bruise on her cheek, watched the colors change, watched it fade. She imagined all the ways she could leave bruises of her own.

Did she say anything, though? *Do* anything? Of course not.

"My battery's dead," Jessica lamely replied.

It was a bad lie. John would know. The word *dead* sounded fake, cracked in half.

"I asked her to stay and help," Peter said, rising to stand.

"Let's go," John commanded, ignoring Peter altogether. "What's wrong with your hair, Jess?"

Jessica was still holding the plastic bag of red candy fish. It was the perfect, stupid prop for this scene—this one scene of her entire, stupid life. She closed her eyes, willing the doors inside her to all bang shut. It was time to play dead. Tonight, after they left here, John would get pissed, then probably want to have sex with her, and she'd probably let him.

After dropping the bag of candy, Jessica stood. John approached her and reached out to brush his hand across her cheek. Jessica looked at Peter, and saw his gaze jumping from the bruise on her cheek to John's thumb. He didn't even try to hide his open staring. The muscles in Peter's jaw twitched as he noticed how they matched—the size and shape of John's thumb and the size and shape of the mark on Jessica's face. Jessica turned away and grasped John's hand in hers before Peter could catch her eye or say anything. She didn't want be on the receiving end of his rage or his pity. She didn't want anything from him. She didn't care if he was leaving in a couple of days, and she wasn't going to sign his fucking card.

But then Jessica did something she couldn't really explain. On her way down the aisle, she grabbed a couple of chocolate truffles and stuffed them in her pocket. She hoped that Peter had seen her. Maybe he'd take it as a reminder that she was a bad influence. Or maybe she wanted him to know that, in a way, she'd be carrying a little piece of him in her pocket for a while.

The Night Jessica Torres
Made Out with John Chavez
in Front of Everyone

IT WAS THE first party we'd ever been to.

That's not true, of course. We'd been to plenty of birthday parties, block parties, baptisms, but this was different.

It was the first party we'd ever been to where we'd walked in, stood among the kids we went to school with, and felt like the smallest people in the world. Not small in stature, but small in spirit. We'd done everything, of course, to try to make that not be the case. We'd planned it to where we walked into Evalin Uvalde's house on that Friday night in the early days of September, three months after Ana had died, like a pack, like a gang, with blasé-sneering expressions on our faces, intentionally two and a half hours late, dressed in our coolest clothes and wearing too much cologne. The goal was to make an impression while pretending like we didn't care about making an impression. When we walked into Evalin's house, however, we made absolutely no impression. None. People may have looked at us, but they didn't see us. They looked *through* us. We were wallpaper.

The very first thing we saw when we walked into Evalin's house was Evalin herself. John Chavez had her pressed up against the wall of the entryway—right inside the front door—and they were really going at it. Behind them and around them were tons of people drinking, laughing, and shout-talking into each other's ears. All those people were acting like it was no big deal that John had one hand up Evalin's shirt and was full-on groping her boob. Honestly, it kind of looked painful for Evalin, like John was squeezing the way someone might furiously juice an orange. And the sounds their mouths were making were so weird and loud. There were people laughing and shouting, there was music playing, but even still, over all that, we could hear the squish and slide and suck of lips and tongue. None of us had *that* much experience with making out—Hector claimed to have gotten to "third base" with Faye Gutierrez after the block party two summers ago, though Hector was very often full of shit—but what was going on between John and Evalin seemed super unromantic.

We were grossed out, but that didn't mean we could

stop staring. Eventually, Calvin elbowed Hector. Hector blinked and elbowed Jimmy. It was time to snap out of it and move. We turned ourselves sideways and started inching through the crowd. Of course, we knew that if we were in any way as cool as we had hoped we'd be, the crowd would've parted for *us*.

The last time we were in such a full house was when we were at Hector's on the afternoon after Ana's funeral. We'd been on a mission then: to gather up precious bits of information about Ana. This party at Evalin's wasn't at all the same, and we had a completely different, three-part mission: to convince the people we went to school with we weren't total losers, to get tipsy on cheap beer, and to maybe talk to some girls. We kept our ears open, though. Maybe people were still talking about Ana; maybe she was still, in a way, alive to these people—like she was for us—in the swirls of stories and rumors.

For sure, Ana would've been in this house, at this party, if she'd been alive. She would've snuck out her window to get here. All the kids from school would've stopped what they were doing the moment she came through the door. They would've turned and looked. The noise level would've lowered. The crowd would've parted for her as she moved through it. There seemed to be a big, black hole in the middle of Evalin's house where Ana should've been.

Did anyone aside from us think that? For sure, John Chavez didn't.

See, there's something else about John—something big, something we learned later from the other kids at school. John was the guy who Ana had been sneaking out her window to see on the nights leading up to her death. John was the guy who Ana had been sneaking out her window to see on *the* night of her death. John had watched Ana slip, Ana fall, Ana hit the ground. And he'd *driven away*. He wasn't the villain in our story because villains typically have spines. He was lower than that—the ultimate, ultimate unrepentant coward.

From what we'd just witnessed in the entryway, John had very clearly moved on, and we didn't understand how. That was a huge part of why we couldn't stop staring when we'd first walked in. We were sort of transfixed, but we were also really, really pissed—even though John was known far and wide to be a grade-A dick, the more we thought about it, the more it made us slow-burn angry how he'd moved on, and with Evalin Uvalde of all people.

Evalin had a long-standing reputation for being really mean. Jessica Torres was also mean, but the two were mean in different ways. We'd always thought Jessica was mean because she was so full of life that it chafed at her from the inside out. She was always simmering, and it reminded us of a pot of stew on a stove. She contained so much beneath her skin, and when she got heated up, all those things tumbled and boiled. Evalin, on the other hand, was colder, crueler. She'd say and do mean things just to say and do mean things. Evalin was the type of person who would trip a kid to watch them cry and then deny ever having done anything—and then tell the kid it was *their* fault.

Less than ten minutes after we'd arrived at the party, Jessica Torres finally showed up. We ran into her when she was in the kitchen, by herself, pouring Sprite and vodka into a red plastic cup. She was wearing Ana's clothes—a black denim skirt that didn't fit quite right and an oversized blue T-shirt—but she was always wearing Ana's clothes those days, so that wasn't surprising. The cup she was holding was shaking because her hand was shaking. Her hair was tied back, and we could see pink splotches on her cheeks. She was about to pop. We'd seen her look that way, at Hector's house, right before she attacked Father Canty. If Jessica had come in through the front door, she would have seen what we'd seen: John Chavez swallowing Evalin's face like a desperate fish.

"Hey, Jessica," Calvin said, trying to sound cool and casual. "Are you okay? Do you need anything?"

Jessica's gaze flashed up, and Calvin winced. He actually cowered a little, as if the rage on Jessica's face caused him real pain.

"What the fuck did you just say?" Jessica snapped.

"He just wanted to know if you're okay," Jimmy chimed in. He waited a couple seconds before adding, "Are you?"

For a few terrible moments, Jessica studied us, and we waited for whatever insults she would spear our way. We braced ourselves. We were ready. It would be okay. We'd welcome those insults because we knew whatever pain they would cause us would be temporary and would pale in comparison to the pain that constantly tumbled and boiled through Jessica's organs.

The insults never came, though. After a moment, Jessica let out a sound—like a breath or a grunt, a noise that indicated we weren't even worth the effort of forming a word—and then she tipped her head back to expose the length of her throat, chugged her drink, and reached back to the bottles perched on the kitchen counter to pour herself another. She took great care to fill her cup up to the very tip-top, and then walked out.

We followed Jessica through the crowd of people, and, to her credit, she managed not to spill more than a couple of drops of her drink. She was headed to the entryway, to where John and Evalin were still doing their thing and John *still* had his hand squashed against Evalin's boob.

Jessica was mad, and when she was mad she created something like a force field of anger. People stopped talking and turned in her direction. They made space for her as she slid by. We heard someone whisper, "Oh shit," and just as Evalin tore her swollen lips away from John's mouth, Jessica threw—overhand threw like a baseball—her cup straight at Evalin's face. The plastic and ice and clear liquid exploded against Evalin's nose. The cup bounced off John's shoulder.

"*What the fuck, bitch?*" Evalin screeched, as John just backed off, eyes wide, shaking himself dry and lifting the edge of his shirt to wipe the side of his face.

We tensed, waiting. All around us, others did the same. Jessica was going to do something. She was going to either say something brutal or strike out violently, like the way she'd done with the priest or the way she'd done with Muriel Contreras and the pencil. We watched, not caring anymore about being cool, but wanting to know how Jessica was going to avenge her dead sister. We silently cheered her on.

Evalin wiped her face with her hand. She lunged off the wall and shoved Jessica in the shoulder.

"I said, *What the fuck?*"

Do it, Jessica, we urged. *Make things right.*

Jessica drew in a sharp breath, and then she did . . . nothing. More like, she shrunk. All of a sudden, her body seemed to get much, much smaller. Her eyes stopped glowing with rage and went dull, out like a light—*click*. We'd always known Jessica Torres as a fighter, but that night we watched her lose that fight. Something in her just gave up. Evalin shoved Jessica again on the shoulder, and Jessica lazily swiped Evalin's hand away. Evalin, obviously embarrassed, screamed in Jessica's face about Jessica being pathetic, about Jessica's *family* being pathetic, and that new version of blank Jessica stood there, staring first at the wall just over Evalin's shoulder and then over to John Chavez.

It was one of the many times we could have said or done something and, instead, we said and did nothing. One of Evalin's friends eventually came over, straightened Evalin's shirt that was still all bunched from having John's hand up it, and started to pull Evalin into the other room.

Jessica was still staring at John, with that cold dullness in her eyes, and John was now staring back. The side of his mouth quirked up. Jessica took a step forward. She then pressed herself flat against John's chest and took hold of both sides of his face. From the other room, Evalin could see what was going on. She shouted out, enraged, as Jessica stood on the tips of her toes and crushed her lips against John's.

She was the one who then pressed John back against the wall of the entryway, and *she* was the one who put her hand up *his* shirt. Their lips and tongues slid and smacked against each other.

"What the hell?" Hector whispered.

Jessica and John have been together ever since.

Jessica

(Saturday, June 15th)

A SCREECHY LAUGH from across the street made Jessica flinch. That laugh, so piercing and distinct as to rise above a big crowd, belonged to Norma Galván, Rafe's date to the block party. As Rafe flipped burgers at a portable grill set up in the Garcias' front yard, Norma laughed at every single thing he said. And, as Norma laughed, she had to fight to keep her balance because the high heels of her strappy sandals kept sinking into the lawn. In between bursts of laughter and trying to stay upright, Norma took sips from a can of Tecate and picked at her flower-printed blouse in an attempt to separate the fabric from her moist skin. Jessica watched as Rafe leaned down toward Norma and nuzzled his nose at her temple. Norma gazed up, smiling all loopy.

Jessica was standing next to John in the shade of an oak tree, wondering if she'd ever looked at him all loopy like that. She also wondered why her father was hanging out with Norma Galván again. Possibly, it had to do with money, given that Rafe had asked Jessica the other day to "borrow" two hundred dollars. Norma was known to keep rolls of cash stashed all over her house, in places like coffee cans and hollow porcelain statues. Rafe had said he needed the money for a truck payment, but Jessica was pretty sure his truck had been paid off for years.

Jessica then heard a different laugh—gentle like skipping stones—and she knew exactly who that laugh belonged to because she'd heard it dozens of times from across the store, from aisles away. There, behind a couple of folding tables covered with foil-wrapped dishes, was Peter. He was helping Mrs. Garcia pour tea into red plastic cups and was grinning at a little boy who was not-so-sneakily trying to steal three cookies off a plate.

Next to Peter was Calvin Ortiz's mom, who was fussing over things, making sure everything was all set, that there were enough paper plates, napkins, forks, and spoons. She smacked the boy's hand away from the cookies, but laughed while she did it. In a nearby yard, Kitty Bolander and her friends were having a Hula-Hoop contest. The girls were laughing so loud, they sounded like they were screaming, like their joy took up so much space in their bodies it was physically painful.

It was a bright, beautiful, non-rainy day, and there was laughter everywhere. No one knew that the ghost of Ana Torres had caused Iridian to freeze in place on the downstairs couch, or that Jessica hadn't slept any more than eight hours combined over the course of the last three days. Jessica was surprised no one could see how badly she was starting to warp. Everything—her vision, her attention span, her ability to sort change into the register—felt like pencil marks that had been half-heartedly rubbed out with an eraser. Like everything was as blurry as the letters on old, slumped tombstones or like the shadow outline of a hand against a shower curtain.

No one in the neighborhood knew anything about this—about Jessica, about the things happening in Jessica's house. Jessica didn't really want anyone to know. She cringed. She felt like she was under assault.

Teddy Arenas's new dog, a sand-colored, big-pawed puppy, bounded up to John and started pulling on the end of his shoelace with his tiny, determined teeth. John smiled and crouched down. He made cooing sounds and let the dog lick him on his hands and his nose, even on his lips. Eventually, the puppy rolled onto his back and gazed all goo-goo-eyed at John the way Norma was gazing at Rafe across the street.

Jessica told herself: John is a good person because he likes dogs. Good people like dogs.

But then Jessica realized she was still cringing. The expression was stuck on her face. Just as Teddy came up to reclaim his dog, Jessica heard Peter's stone-skip laugh again, and turned to the sound. She knew she didn't smile, but it was possible that her expression had softened.

"I'm going to get something to drink," Jessica said before heading over to the table where Mrs. Garcia and Peter were still setting up cups of iced tea. John had seen it: the way Jessica had reacted to Peter's laugh. She knew because even though she hadn't asked John to follow her, she could sense him close behind, and she knew what he'd do before he did it. He reached out and took hold of Jessica's wrist, stopping her mid-step. He squeezed so that his fingers dug into the place right at Jessica's pulse point, and her whole arm tensed. She winced as a ribbon of pain shot up to her elbow.

"Time to go," John said, without raising his voice.

Jessica let out a huff but stayed rooted. Behind her, Kitty Bolander and her friends were still shrieking their joy. Again, Jessica looked over to her dad and Norma.

Norma was stroking a hand up and down Rafe's arm, lightly. She then threaded her fingers with the ones on his free hand and leaned in to rest her cheek against his shoulder. Norma gave Rafe a kiss on his temple, so tenderly it nearly made Jessica gasp. She was transfixed. She couldn't stop watching this woman, her neighbor yet a stranger, offer comfort to her father.

Jessica was jealous. She wished she had someone who would hold her hand in a gentle way and lean against her shoulder. She even wished she was a dog so that John would take her face in his hands and gaze at her like she was the sweetest thing in the world. Instead, John was still gripping her wrist with so much force her fingers were starting to go numb.

"Did you not hear me?" John asked. He tugged her wrist, down, and Jessica felt her shoulder jerk out of joint. "I said, it's time to go."

Jessica watched a squirrel drop an acorn into a tiny hole at the base of a tree in a neighbor's front yard. She wished she was at work, under the freezing-cold air-conditioning, stocking candy and humming along to ballads. She wished she was alone in her car, singing at the top of her lungs. Jessica said nothing, and pretended her silence was a revolutionary act. She then realized how sad that was.

"I fucking heard you," Jessica muttered.

She ripped her hand from John's grip and continued toward the tables. But John reached out again, grabbing her by the elbow this time. He was trying to get her to stop, of course, but also to turn and face him.

Jessica didn't do that. She didn't look over her shoulder at John because she had the buzzy feeling of being watched. She turned her head slightly and locked eyes with Peter. He was still behind the folding table. Only now, he wasn't filling cups. He was holding one, though, and Jessica watched the plastic buckle under the strain of his grip. His gaze moved from Jessica's eyes to her elbow—and to John's hand there. A muscle twitched at the narrow edge of his eyebrow.

John squeezed tighter, and Jessica sagged a little from the sudden hit of pain. She knew that John had seen Peter looking at Jessica. He knew what Peter saw, and that's why he'd squeezed harder. In the past—like, a couple of days ago—Jessica would've been scared. She would've anticipated anger and then pain, and it would've made her weak with fear. Not today, though. Not on this bright and beautiful day. Peter's eyebrow twitched again, and Jessica sucked in a breath.

She didn't know exactly what would happen next, but she had an idea. She lifted her free hand to cover a smile.

"What the fuck are you looking at?" John sneered at Peter.

Peter leapt over the table, knocking over several cups and sending their contents splashing. He shoved John, not on the shoulder or on the chest, but on the face—like, he put his *entire hand* on John's face and pushed it backwards, chin to sky. John stumbled but recovered, and then quickly landed a punch on Peter's left eye.

Hector and Calvin were sprinting across the street—to do what, Jessica had no idea. This amazing fight didn't need to end, and Peter didn't need any help. A line of blood was trailing down the side of Peter's face—just like that line of sweat from a few days ago in the parking lot—but Jessica didn't have the urge to go up and wipe it away. She liked it. Liked the way it started at his brow and traced his cheekbone. She also liked it when Peter grabbed John by the front of his shirt and punched him in the nose. The resulting crunch was loud and oddly inhuman, like a grunt a dog makes when it launches itself into a bowl of food. John landed hard against one of the folding tables. Plates and serving bowls flew, and the table itself crashed to the ground.

It took a moment, but when John stood, he was covered in a swirl of food and blood. His white T-shirt was smeared with red but also something brown—chocolate cake, maybe—and a deviled egg was stuck, yolk-side, to his upper arm. John lumbered toward Peter, fists clenched. The blood on Peter's face had reached his chin. Then it dripped—so perfectly—right onto the toe of Peter's off-white sneaker. Peter didn't notice. He didn't blink, didn't back down, as John lunged.

Peter ducked. He elbowed John in the stomach, and when John doubled over, Peter punched him underhand. Again, blood sprayed, Corvette red, into the grass and onto Peter's sneakers. John straightened, and Jessica noticed the skin around his eyes was already turning colors.

And what was Jessica doing all this time? She was just standing there. She wasn't trying to pull John away or yelling for them to stop or anything. Ice and iced tea had sprayed onto her at some point, but she'd made no effort to wipe it off. Her hand had moved from her mouth, her fingers splayed across her nose and her eyes. She was doing that thing, faking horror, watching while pretending not to be watching. But if someone were to take a closer look, they'd see her cheekbones hiking up and gentle crinkles around the corners of her eyes, like she was smiling and trying to cover up her glee. Like she was *laughing*.

And where was Rafe? He was still behind the grill, watching. Norma was huddled up against him. A spatula hung from one hand. Jessica glanced his way and thought he looked kind of limp, kind of frightened, like the last thing he'd ever want to do was leap into the fray and break up a fight between two young men. That's the kind of man Rafe Torres was—the kind who would cling to a spatula in a time of crisis. Even Hector and Calvin had finally decided to step in and were now attempting to pry John and Peter away from each other.

Jessica couldn't hold it in anymore. She laughed. The sound burst out of her, and it sounded harsh and mean, like a row of grackles squawking on a telephone wire. She didn't think she'd ever laughed like that before. Clearly, she was losing her mind. She laughed and laughed.

Calvin and Hector were pulling John away from Peter, and John kept yelling, "I will fucking kill you!" which somehow made Jessica laugh harder. There were tears in her eyes. Her vision blurred. She started hiccupping. She doubled over, clutching her stomach, and eventually landed on her knees in the grass. The sun was still shining on this bright, cloudless day. It was hot, but the grass was cool, and the ground beneath was soft.

Jessica collapsed onto her side, and it was like she was a tiny bug peering through the tall blades of grass. She felt as if she could laugh there forever.

Rosa

ALMOST EXACTLY TWO years ago, Rosa and Ana had been sitting together on their back porch, doing nothing special, just drinking iced tea on a warm summer night. Even if they never had anything to talk about, since they were so far apart in age, Rosa had always liked being alone with her oldest sister. She liked that they shared an appreciation of the dark sky, and she liked the way Ana's long hair was always wavy and dynamic, like it was caught on a breeze even if there was no breeze at all.

There had been fireflies that night, blinking at the edges of the yard, and as time passed, the fireflies had multiplied. There were still some in the distance, but others were lighting up just inches away from Rosa's face. Ana had been reaching out and lazily trying to grab them. More and more had started blinking—so many that they'd played tricks with Rosa's vision, leaving tracks and trails, the way fireworks do.

"Are you doing this?" Ana had asked Rosa, and in the next moment, the yard went dark. The fireflies had blinked out, all at the same time, but Rosa could still feel them there, hovering in the heavy air. She could hear the hum of their little wings.

"You *are*," Ana had said, and then the yard had burst with light, so suddenly that it made Rosa gasp. The fireflies had lit up, all together. Then, a long moment later, they'd gone back to their regular, irregular blinking.

"I didn't," Rosa had said. "I'm not."

"I've always known there was something special about you," Ana had replied. She'd said it sternly, like a schoolteacher. "Now we know."

No one had ever said anything like that to Rosa before. It would've seemed like a tacky, bad-luck thing to say. Rosa had never thought there'd been something special about her. In fact, she'd thought there'd been something very sad about her. Her life was the cause of someone else's death. She'd been born, and her mother had died. It was a simple and terrible fact.

"Listen," Ana had said. "You're different than everyone

else. You're blessed. I mean, God has gifted you with something. I don't know what it is, but it's something. I hope you figure out what it is. I hope you can make the fireflies do that again."

Rosa

(Saturday, June 15th)

ROSA WAS WALKING to Concepcion Park when she heard shouting, followed by the crunching and crashing of things colliding. She hustled back toward home and saw that Peter Rojas and John Chavez were fighting. People had gathered around. Jessica was in the grass, on her back. She looked like she was convulsing. Rosa ran to her sister and saw that Jessica wasn't convulsing. She was laughing.

"Girls?" Mrs. Bolander asked, tentatively approaching. "Is everything alright?"

"We're fine," Rosa said, putting her hand on her sister's shoulder. "Jessica? What happened?"

Jessica couldn't respond. She was gripping her stomach, hardly able to breathe, overcome by her cackles.

The shouting and crashing and crunching continued just a few feet away. Rosa didn't look, but she could hear the sound of flesh thwacking against flesh, followed by stupid John telling Peter he would kill him. Jessica laughed harder.

Rosa glanced up just in time to see Peter punch John in the eye. The blood was so red as it left John's body. Red like the feathers of the cardinal that had fallen from the tree.

Iridian

(Saturday, June 15th)

IRIDIAN HADN'T UNDERSTOOD the sunlight at first.
She'd woken up on the couch after a nap of hours or minutes, licked her dry lips, and stretched out from fingertip
to toe before she'd noticed the long rays of light seeping in
through the curtains. The light caused her to sit straight
up, and that's when she saw the notebook on her lap. It was
new. She could tell without even opening it. The cover was
yellow plastic, but it had a paper half-cover on top of that,
one that boasted the brand name and page count. Iridian
knew it was a gift from Jessica because when she picked it
up, a receipt from the pharmacy showing a twenty-percent
employee discount fell out.

Iridian held her new notebook for a moment before flipping through the crisp, blank pages. Some were stuck together. They smelled beautiful, fresh like ink and chemicals.

Laughter from the block party outside filtered through the walls of the house. Iridian's sisters had suggested earlier that she get out, if just for a little while, if just for a hot dog and a piece of Mrs. Bolander's famous buttermilk pie, but Iridian would rather stay inside with a ghost than go outside with actual living people and animals and who knew what else. She went to the kitchen to grab a snack and maybe even make herself a cup of tea. Even though she spent most of her time indoors, Iridian could appreciate a nice day. The sun was shining after several dreary days of rain. There were breezes. Iridian couldn't feel them, of course, but she could see the leaves and the branches of the trees swaying, and she watched a squirrel chase another squirrel across the abandoned frame of the trundle bed in the dirt yard. It was all very simple. Bad things didn't happen on a day like this, when the sky was bright and people were outside laughing.

As she smacked on her chocolate puffs, Iridian surveyed the kitchen—the cracked and stained linoleum floor; the loud, whining appliances that had probably come with the house back in the 1970s; the fridge that randomly released ice cubes from its door; the food-spattered range.

It made her think: This house isn't good enough to be haunted. There weren't any libraries with old, cryptic notes shoved between the yellowing pages of dusty books. There weren't winding staircases with polished banisters. There weren't wood floors that were warm and worn from the soles of many generations of family feet. There weren't any gables or widow's walks or turrets. There weren't any rooms that were a little bit colder than the others, or rooms that were kept locked up "just in case." The walls didn't moan when the wind blew. The Torres family wasn't entangled in some generational curse like the Mayfair witches. They had no important heirlooms, just a banker's box full of their mom's old stuff that their dad kept on a shelf in his closet. It contained a couple of button-up blouses, a pair of red flat shoes, a bundle of crepe-paper flowers, a recipe book that used to belong to Grandmamá de la Cruz, and a postcard their mother had once sent home from a trip she took to see family in Morelia, Michoacán.

There were piles of dirty laundry in the closets and unwashed dishes in the kitchen sink. The faucet in Iridian's bathtub always dripped, and there was a ring of rust around the drain. Jessica didn't even have a real shower curtain, just a plastic liner that was once clear but was now streaked with layers of mineral deposits and grime. Everywhere, the carpet was old and dirty. Some of it was buckling, wrinkled like waves on water. Not a single bed in the house was made. The furniture was practically all from estate sales. The house was just some crappy old house, not in any way ghost-worthy.

Iridian knew that if she died on the couch or from falling down the stairs, and had any kind of choice in the matter, she would never, ever stick around this place.

Again, laughter rose up from outside. There was the shrieking of little kids doing something like chasing each other around. Then Iridian heard a woman's gleeful *whoop*, followed by a man shouting *Hey!* to someone.

People were happy. They deserved their nice party. If Iridian were there, things would only get worse. She'd be forced into talking to someone. She would probably say the wrong thing.

The spoon Iridian had been using to eat her cereal slipped from her fingers and fell with a clang into her bowl. The milk tasted acidic. She gagged, nearly choking on mushy chocolate puff.

Even now, a year later, she could still feel the sudden, vibrant shame she'd felt after saying the wrong thing to Ana, just hours before she died. It felt like a full-body rumble, an *oh shit* shock followed by the intense desperation of wanting to scoop words back into her mouth and eat them.

The day Ana fell from her window, she and Iridian had fought. It started when Iridian went into Ana's bathroom to borrow some shampoo. At the time, Ana had been downstairs in the kitchen with Jessica—Iridian could hear them both laughing, followed by the sound of one of them mashing the buttons on the microwave. As Iridian had been leaving with the shampoo bottle in hand, she'd seen that one of Ana's drawers was open. Normally, whatever was crammed in a drawer wouldn't have caught Iridian's eye—decades' worth of anything and everything filled every corner of the Torres house—but what she'd seen made her heart plummet.

It was a pregnancy test. It was new, unopened, safe in its box. But still.

There were footsteps on the stairs, and Iridian heard her sister—Ana—call out her name.

For a moment, Iridian considered acting like nothing had happened and nothing was wrong. She could slide the drawer all the way closed and Ana would never know about her snooping. But Iridian didn't want to act like nothing had happened. Of course, she knew Ana snuck out her window all the time to meet boys, but she never would've guessed her sister would be so careless—so *stupid*—as to get herself pregnant, or in a situation where she might even *think* she was pregnant.

It was a nightmare. Iridian saw it all unfold. She knew Ana would have the baby. It would be a little girl because this was a house full of girls, and all Iridian's plans of running away with her sisters would be ruined. They couldn't run with a baby. Ana couldn't be both their leader and a mother. None of the rest of them could be the leader. Iridian wasn't brave enough—not brave like girls in books.

Jessica could make a decision but could never follow through with anything. Rosa would just lead them in circles.

Iridian had sucked the end of her braid into her mouth, hoping to taste the faint tang of the dirt from the South Texas orange groves. Instead, she'd tasted oil and sweat—it wasn't the same at all.

Iridian took the box from the drawer. She held the tragedy in her hand, and when Ana finally reached the top of the stairs and found her, Iridian said, "You said we'd go back. You *told* us."

"Go back where?" Ana asked. Her gaze fell to the box in Iridian's hand. "Iridian, wait."

Iridian didn't wait. Instead she hurled out the ugliest thing she could think of—a thing that was not true, but true in that moment. "How could you do this to us, you dumb whore?"

Ana slammed the bathroom door shut and leapt forward.

"You're going through my stuff?" Ana demanded, all up in Iridian's face.

Iridian waited—to get smacked, to be yelled at, for Ana to get defensive and then apologize and apologize again—but Ana just crumbled. She fell back against the closed door, covered her eyes, and sobbed. Eventually, Ana slid all the way down to the ground and tossed the pregnancy test across the bathroom. Iridian was trapped.

All she could do was stand there, mortified, radiant with shame. She did swallow, a couple of times, as if trying to gulp down her sour-tasting mistake. At last, Iridian took a step toward her sister, but Ana held up a hand, silently commanding Iridian to stay back.

"I was so scared," Ana hiccupped. She wiped her eyes roughly. "But it's nothing. It's fine now. *You're* fine now, Iridian. Alright?"

Again, Iridian took a step forward. She reached out, but her sister smacked her hand away.

"No," Ana said. "You fucked up."

Ana stood and left, and those were the last words Iridian ever heard her sister say.

The laughter continued outside as Iridian spit out her half-chewed cereal, rinsed out her bowl, and put it in the overstuffed dishwater. The front door opened, and there was a new sound—gaspy and raspy, a sort of hysterical giggling. It belonged to Jessica. When was the last time Iridian had heard Jessica *giggle*? When had she *ever* heard her do that?

"What's going on?" Iridian asked, stepping into the living room.

"There was a fight," Rosa replied. Jessica was collapsed against her little sister, gripping Rosa's shoulders to keep from falling over. She was wet, like someone had tripped and spilled a drink on her shirt. "Between John and Peter Rojas."

Jessica laughed harder.

Iridian looked to Rosa to explain, but all Rosa could do was shrug and shake her head. After a few seconds, Jessica managed to get herself together enough to head toward the staircase on her own.

"Are you sure you're okay?" Iridian asked.

Jessica hiccupped. "I just need to change clothes." She hiccupped again.

Jessica got halfway up the stairs, and then spun toward her sisters. Her head had swiveled so fast, it looked like she'd been hit in the face. She wasn't laughing anymore.

"Wh—?" Iridian started.

She couldn't finish the question because she didn't want the answer. There had to be something else, some new terrible thing—phantom steps on the stairs, a misplaced, girl-shaped figure in a doorway, or more writing on the walls—more *I want*s. Iridian reached back to grip the couch and dug her nails into its scratchy fibers.

Jessica shook her head and tapped her ear.

That meant: *Listen.*

There was still the sound of laughter coming from outside, but new laughter had joined it. It was different: joyful, rising like a cluster of bubbles, but also sort of cruel and breathy and gleeful. It was the sound of someone who'd just been told a good-bad secret. It was as familiar as the handwritten letter *a*'s on the wall. It was Ana's laugh, and it was coming from upstairs, in the direction of Jessica's bedroom.

Jessica spun again and then ran down the stairs. Halfway down, she tripped over an old tear in the carpet and was thrown into a waiting Rosa.

The laughter continued, and Iridian cried out. She turned and braced herself—her hands and her forehead—against the back edge of the couch. She pressed hard. She was trying to get *in*.

"Stop!" Jessica commanded. *"Shut up."*

The laughing stopped. There were still the squeals coming from the little kids outside, but the house was quiet. Iridian stayed where she was, scraping her face against the couch. She felt her sister—Rosa—reach out and put a cool, small hand on her back. The three Torres sisters waited. Outside, a couple of birds chirped, thrilled about the sunshine.

Iridian heard Jessica swallow hard and then say, "Ana?"

There was a creak, like a foot being placed on the top step, followed by a drawn-out, hungry inhale, the type that someone would take after having held their breath under-water for a long, long time.

Iridian yelled, then yelled again. She kept yelling, over and over—long, loud, incoherent, non-word cries. She was yelling because she didn't want to hear what came after that inhale. She wanted the sound of her yelling to rise up and swallow the sounds of her sister's spirit. She wanted to drown out the world with noise.

Jessica
(Saturday, June 15th)

JESSICA LEFT THE house—she bolted out the door and was gone. The maniacal laughter that had felt like big, big waves crashing against the walls of her stomach, pressing against her rib cage, had been replaced by dead-cold nothing. She was a void. Iridian was yelling with her face smashed against the cushions, and Jessica didn't want to hear that. Rosa would take care of it.

Jessica found John right outside, leaning against her car, holding a cup of ice to his beat-up face. Peter was nowhere around, and his truck wasn't parked outside Hector's anymore.

"Where'd you go?" he asked.

"To change," she replied.

John looked to the front of Jessica's shirt, which was still speckled with light brown drops.

"Come on," she said, unlocking the door.

Jessica could do these easy things: walk out of her house, unlock her car door, drive to the pharmacy, buy first aid supplies to fix up John's face. These things were simple, as opposed to going back into her house and listening to her dead sister laugh with her or *at* her or whatever the fuck that was.

John waited in the car while Jessica went into the pharmacy to buy antiseptic and cotton balls. After that, she administered first aid in the parking lot. The cut on John's lip was crusted with blood, and she could tell from the bruising it probably still smarted. She repeated the simple process: slosh a cotton ball with antiseptic and press to John's lip. Eventually, John bucked his head back and hissed. He reached up and grabbed Jessica's wrist, forcing her to stop and meet his gaze. She tried not to stare at the one eye that was swollen nearly shut, the bruising around it nearly black. The seam of that eye, all along his lashes, was moist, weeping like a cut blister.

"You're pressing too hard," John said.

"Sorry," Jessica muttered.

She wasn't sorry.

Rosa
(Saturday, June 15th)

AFTER WARMING UP some leftover chicken fried rice Jessica had brought home the other day, Rosa eventually coaxed Iridian into the kitchen. They ate together at the table, and then Rosa led Iridian to the couch in the living room. She clicked on the lamp. The television was still on. Rosa sat down next to Iridian and started telling her about her searches for the hyena and her trips up and down the river and out to Concepcion Park. She described the sounds of frogs and wind and crickets.

As Rosa started in on all the birds she'd seen recently—cardinals, bluebirds, crows, little warblers—Iridian's eyelids started to flutter closed.

She waited a few minutes to make sure Iridian was asleep, turned off the television, and then went upstairs to grab a box she kept under her bed. When she was younger, Rosa used to collect all kinds of colorful things. She liked tiny racecars with missing wheels, swirled-glass marbles, and bird feathers. She'd find objects around the neighborhood and hide them all over: in a plastic grocery bag that hung on a hook in her closet, in the hollow of the oak tree outside, in an old sour cream container she'd buried under the bushes in the backyard. Over time, she'd narrowed her collection down to the most important objects, and those objects were in a single shoebox.

Rosa pulled that box onto her lap and sifted through the contents. Her fingers skimmed a fake pearl button and a couple of Fiesta pins, and then landed on the note she'd received last July, a little over a month after Ana had died, from the boys across the street. One of them had written it, printing in very neat letters on a piece of a rounded-edged page from a composition book, the kind Iridian had always used. It was dark in the room, so she couldn't read those neat letters, but she didn't need to read it. She knew by heart what it said.

We saw Ana last night. She was standing in the front yard tapping on your dad's window. We thought you'd want to know. P.S. This is not a joke. We are serious.

She'd believed the boys, figuring they didn't have a reason to lie. They'd never been the mean types. She'd never heard about any of them playing pranks on other kids at their school. They didn't come right out and say they'd seen a ghost, but they didn't have to. She knew that's what had happened. But she couldn't understand why Ana would appear first to Hector and his friends, as opposed to her and her sisters.

There had to be a connection, Rosa thought, between Ana and the hyena and the cardinals. There just had to be. Rosa decided she needed to search again, and she needed a better, or quicker, method than on foot. She needed a car, or someone with a car. There was no way Jessica would take her around, or her dad, but maybe there was another option.

Rosa tucked the boys' note back in with the pearl button and the pins and the rest of her most important treasures. She guided the box to its hiding place, and then went into the hall to grab the receiver to the landline. She tried the church first, but Walter Mata wasn't there. He picked up on the second ring on his home phone.

"Hi, it's Rosa Torres," she said. "Do you think you can borrow your mom's car for a while?"

Rosa was wondering if she'd made a mistake. Cars were different from feet. Obviously. She was too removed from the ground. The car's muffler was sort of broken, making *huff-huff* sounds. Being a cautious driver with only his recently acquired learner's permit, Walter was diligent about using his turn signals, so in the background there were always these little *click-clack*s. The radio was on, playing the doo-wop oldies his mom liked. It was low-volume, but still. Rosa didn't like those kinds of sounds.

"Why do you want to find this hyena so badly?" Walter asked.

"It might need my help." Rosa was looking out the open window. She'd trained her eyes to see in the dark. She could make out distinctions in black shades and shapes and could tell a possum from a cat from a football field away.

"How can you help it?" Walter asked.

"I don't know," Rosa replied. "I'll know when I find it."

She'd had Walter drive her up and down the streets closest to her house first, and they'd fanned out from there. Closer to downtown, just a few streets away from hers, things were changing. Where, a few weeks ago, a small house had sat, there was now an empty lot. Where, a few weeks ago, an empty lot had sat, there was now a new, bigger house, or a small row of condos, or a bar with a cute, cursive neon sign above the door. Several of the houses that were still there had For Sale signs out front, even though those houses were occupied and Rosa could see lights on inside.

"I think it has something to do with my sister," Rosa said. "The hyena, I mean."

"Which sister?"

"Ana."

"Oh. As in, her spirit?"

"Yes." Rosa swiveled in her seat. "You think that makes sense?"

"I know a thing or two about spirits," Walter replied. "I spend a lot of time in an old church, remember?"

Rosa turned again to face the window. "Father Mendoza spends a lot of time in an old church, too, but he hasn't been particularly helpful or encouraging."

"To clarify," Walter said, "I spend a lot of time in the *basements* and *abandoned rooms* of an old church. I have a different perspective."

Rosa smiled out into the night. Maybe, she thought, this trip wasn't a mistake after all.

"Let's try the park again," she said.

Walter clicked on his turn signal.

For almost an hour, Rosa and Walter walked through Concepcion Park. The night wasn't hot, but the air was thick. Rosa was sweating inside her rubber boots, and her dress was sticking to her skin. It turned out to be not a very good night for searching. There were too many distractions. People were out late, playing baseball under the harsh lights. Cars took up almost all of the spaces in the lots. Some of those cars had windows that were steamed up—or smoked up, Rosa couldn't tell. Walter wasn't a distraction, though. Sometimes he tagged along beside Rosa, and sometimes he went his own way. Whenever she looked, Rosa noticed a firefly flash above Walter's right shoulder. She was sure this was a sign, a good omen. She needed a good omen.

"Are you scared?" Walter asked. "About your sister?"

"No," Rosa replied. "I just want to know what she wants. Are *you* scared? Of the spirits in the church?"

"Oh yeah." Walter laughed. "But not enough to quit my job, right? It's funny. I sort of like being scared."

Rosa didn't think it was funny at all. She thought it was wonderful.

They were making their way across a field when Walter stopped and went into a crouch. He'd found something. Rosa squinted, but she couldn't see what it was. Walter straightened, and there, pinched between his fingers, was the tiniest snail shell. It was a perfect coil, and without a single chip. As he turned it, its iridescence gleamed in the moonlight.

"Do you want this?" Walter asked, holding the shell out to Rosa.

"Yes," Rosa replied.

She knew exactly where she'd keep it.

Iridian
(Saturday, June 15th)

ON THIS NIGHT, when Iridian wrote, she was alone in a dark house. The first thing she did was turn the television back on so she could take comfort in the glow of other people's fake lives, and the second thing she did was grab her new notebook. Using a blue pen Rosa had fetched from upstairs earlier, Iridian filled all the lines of the first page with two words: *I'm sorry.*

They were, of course, for Ana—for what Iridian had said a year and a week ago. Apologies and forgiveness were rare and did not come easy in the Torres house, because rarely did anyone deserve them.

Iridian hated emotions because the one she felt the most was shame. It never left, or when she thought it was gone, there it was again, like a hard tap on her shoulder or a sudden stomach cramp or the sound of her name being called when she was sure no one was around. Iridian knew she didn't deserve forgiveness, but Ana deserved apologies. And Iridian would give them to her until her fingers bled. Ana would see them because she had eyes enough to read and then write on walls.

Jessica
(Saturday, June 15th)

AFTER DROPPING JOHN back at his house, Jessica sat in her car in her driveway. It was late, but she still didn't want to go back into her complicated house. Remnants of the block party littered the street. A red plastic cup was wedged in the opening of a storm drain. Several napkins were half stuck to the asphalt, waving feebly in the dull breeze.

Jessica's left arm was draped out her driver's-side window, and she was tapping a beat on her car door. Across the street, the light was on in Hector's bedroom, and she wondered if the boys knew she was out there. Finally, close to midnight, she saw Peter's truck round the corner and pull to a stop in front of Hector's. As Peter killed his engine and opened his door, Jessica whisper-shouted his name and climbed out of her car.

Peter stopped, his eyes narrowed. He looked up and down the darkened street and tossed his keys in his hand, as if he was testing their weight and was ready to use them as a weapon.

"It's just me," Jessica said. "I swear it."

Peter came forward, and Jessica saw the short, neat cut between his left eye and his brow. Aside from that, the eye didn't look so bad. It wasn't swollen shut and oozing fluid, though the white part was shot through with streaks of red, like some capillaries had burst. She quickly scanned the rest of his face. The light from the street lamps was dim and hazy orange, but she couldn't see any swelling at his jaw or bruising at his temple. Jessica wished he would smile one of his easy smiles so she could check if he'd chipped any teeth.

"Here to survey the damage?" Peter's question was an icy snap in the warm night.

"I was worried about you," Jessica replied.

"Why?"

"What do you mean *why*?" Jessica ran her fingers through her humidity-puffed hair and then motioned to the street. "Because of what happened."

"Why would you be worried about me, Jessica?" Peter urged. His face was uncharacteristically stony, nearly eerie under the street lamps. "I'm just someone you work with."

Jessica looked to the street, her eyes landing on what used to be a piece of white frosted cake. It was by the curb, smashed and covered with ants.

"I'm sorry." It was the second time Jessica had said those words that night, but the first time she'd meant them.

Peter stepped closer, and Jessica lifted her gaze from the street just enough to see his hands hanging by his sides. There were bruises on them, across the ridges of the knuckles. Peter flexed his hand, and Jessica wondered how much those knuckle bones still stung, and if anyone had bent over them and cared for them, dabbed gently at them with a cotton ball.

Just inches from Peter's bruised knuckles, a firefly flashed.

"For what?" Peter said. "Sorry for what?"

Jessica startled and looked up. Peter was angry, but he was giving her a chance. She knew that whatever she said next would ruin something. It would either ruin something for her and John, or for her and Peter. She had to make a choice. It wasn't simple. Or, it was too simple.

"Do you want to come inside?" Jessica asked. "We can talk inside."

She could go inside again, if he came with her.

Jessica half expected Peter to glance over his shoulder at Hector's window, to check to see if his friends were watching, but he stayed focused on her.

Did his expression soften, or did Jessica just imagine it?

"Alright." Peter nodded in the direction of the front door. "Sure. After you."

Rafe had always had a rule against boys in the house, but Jessica didn't care about rules right then. Besides, her dad wasn't even home. He was probably out with Norma, spending the night at her not-haunted house. Jessica led Peter through the dimly lit living room, past the flashing television and a sleeping Iridian huddled under that stinky old blanket, and then up to the second floor. On the staircase, Peter slowed to look at the photos in frames that hung on the wall.

"Your mom."

Peter pointed to a photo of Jessica's mother. She was sitting in a lawn chair at a pool party, wearing a forest green bikini and large black sunglasses. Her long brown hair was parted down the middle and hung over her shoulders. Jessica was ready for Peter to ask about her, about how much Jessica remembered about her, and Jessica would have to shrug and say not much, which was the disappointing truth.

"She looks like Rosa," Peter said.

"She does."

Jessica unlocked and opened the door to her bedroom, realizing too late it was an embarrassing wreck of trash and clothes and dirty sheets. Her face turned hot as Peter did a quick scan, taking in the sorry sight of damp towels tossed into corners and empty tubes of lip gloss and mascara that littered the carpet. Nothing in his expression gave away what he might've been thinking until he went to the window, pulled back the curtain, and looked out into the night.

"This used to be Ana's room," Jessica said.

"I knew that." Peter let the curtain drop and then turned toward Jessica. "We used to watch her from Hector's." He dropped his head and shook it. A blush spread across his cheeks. "That sounds creepy. It *was* creepy. We were creeps."

"What did you see?" Jessica asked, genuinely curious.

Peter lifted his head and crinkled his brow.

"When you would watch her," Jessica clarified. "What would she do?"

"She would sneak out," Peter replied. "Climb down the tree. A couple hours later, she'd come back and climb *up* the tree. Most of the time, though, she would just stand here and look out. Not to the street, but to the sky." He paused. "You don't do that. Stand at the window and look out."

Jessica should've been angry. Peter was giving her proof of his and the neighborhood's prying eyes. She wasn't angry, though. There was a difference, she realized, between being spied on and being noticed. She wanted to be noticed, and Peter had noticed her. It gave her a buzzy, soft-edged feeling her hard self wasn't used to.

"Did you see her fall?" Jessica asked.

"No. We heard the glass break. And a car drive away."

"It wasn't John," Jessica said automatically. "He said it wasn't him."

She winced and then scrubbed a hand across her face. It was like those terrible words had actually stung as they came out of her mouth. She'd always known John was there, even if he denied it. The boy who had tasted and touched every centimeter of Jessica's skin had seen her sister die and had driven away.

"I'm sorry," Jessica said. "I'm sorry I just said that."

"You should stop apologizing," Peter said.

Jessica snickered. "Well, I've got a lot to be sorry for, so . . ."

Peter cracked a smile. It was so small, but so perfect. "You weren't the one who decided to fight me."

"All I do is fight you."

Peter opened his mouth to speak but was interrupted by a tapping at the window. The sound wasn't a hollow *ping* made by thrown stones, but more like a softer thud.

A ripple of fear went all the way down Jessica's right arm, from her shoulder and out through her fingers. She closed her eyes and waited for the hard cluck of Ana's laughter.

"The tree?" Peter asked.

Jessica shook her head. "Too far away."

The tapping continued. It was rhythmic and controlled—not like branches being tossed against glass by the unpredictable wind. Jessica opened her eyes and saw that Peter didn't seem scared. He hadn't blanched, and his eyes weren't wide. He went over to the window and pulled back the curtain. The tapping stopped. Peter looked down, to the lawn and to the street, and then turned to face Jessica.

"Ana," she said.

"What does she want?" Peter asked, in an echo of the question Iridian had asked the day before. When Iridian had asked it, Jessica hadn't answered. She hadn't answered because she didn't have an answer. She still didn't.

"I don't know." Jessica sat down on the edge of her unmade bed. "We don't know. It started when I . . . I saw her hand. Then she wrote on the wall. Today, we heard her laughing. I don't know what it means. All these little tricks. It's like . . . why would she do this to us?"

"Do you think she's sending a message?"

"Yes. Maybe. I don't know." Jessica cocked her head. "Do you really believe all this?"

"Sure," Peter said. "Why wouldn't I?"

The way Peter was acting—the way he was standing all easy-like with his hands in his pockets and without his shoulders all tense and hiked up around his ears—it was strange. He'd just been in a street fight and had just been told the room he was standing in was haunted, but somehow that was all no big deal, water off his back.

How, Jessica wondered, can a person not absorb all the cruel and painful and scary things about life? How did Peter not itch every day? How was that possible?

"I haven't told John," Jessica said. "I don't even . . . I don't even know where to start."

Peter didn't respond. Maybe it was because of the mention of John's name.

For a long moment, it was quiet. There was nothing, not the tapping against windows or the rushing hum of the air conditioner. Jessica thought maybe she heard something from downstairs, like Iridian snoring faintly, but then that stopped, too.

"I can't believe you're leaving," Jessica said.

"You can leave too, you know." Peter leaned against the side of Jessica's dresser. "Not many people would choose to stay in a haunted house."

This is what Jessica had wanted: someone to tell her to fly away. And now, here she was, recycling the words that John had spoken a few days ago that had sent her heart plummeting. She was nothing but a mimic.

"I can't leave Southtown. I have a job. My family."

Peter pushed off the dresser and came forward. Jessica wanted so badly to lean forward and do something simple, like lift the edge of his shirt and kiss the skin of his stomach.

"I don't know what it's like to live in this house," Peter said, "and I'm in no position to tell you how to live your life."

"But?"

"But . . ." Peter began. "If I was the ghost of someone who had always, in life, looked out her window with an expression on her face like she was desperate to escape, and I had come back to send a message, it would be to tell her sisters to get out of this house and never look back."

Jessica waited—for the sound against the window to return more urgently, for the light bulbs in her room to burn bright then blow out, for anything big and bold to tell her Peter was right.

"There's one more thing," Peter went on to say, "and I don't care if you repeat it to your boyfriend."

"I won't tell—"

"I don't care if you tell him," Peter said, interrupting. "There are two huge tragedies here. The first is that you are legions better than John Chavez, and he doesn't deserve you."

Jessica's hands balled into fists.

"And the second?" she urged.

"The second is worse. You know you're better than him, but you refuse, for whatever reason, to do anything about it. I have no problem fighting him. I'll do it over and over again, but you should figure out a way to fight him, too. You don't have to do it alone, but you have to do it."

The words were on the tip of Jessica's tongue: *You don't know me. You don't know what you're talking about. Things aren't so fucking easy.*

But also these words: *I still sing. I do it when I'm alone in my car in empty parking lots. My voice is better than it's ever been.*

Jessica closed her eyes, and her ears tuned in to the wheezing rattle of her dad's truck, coming up the street. Soon there was the sound of a steel door slamming shut, followed by a wet, uncovered cough. Jessica opened her eyes, and Peter was there, still hovering in front of her.

"My dad's home," she said. "You should probably go."

Jessica walked Peter out of the house in silence, but once they were out in the yard, Peter stopped and turned.

"I can't hear," he said.

"What?"

"I can't hear anymore," Peter replied. "Not like I used to."

Jessica realized he was answering a question she'd asked when she'd been flat on her back on the floor of a church: *Do you still sing?*

"I was in a fight," Peter said. "I was drunk, and I picked a fight with my sister's boyfriend over nothing, and he hit me in the ear and broke some bones behind my eardrum. I can't find pitch anymore."

"I never heard about that," Jessica said.

"I'm glad." Peter looked out to the empty street. "It's not exactly my proudest moment. And I don't want people thinking I'm a violent drunk, which apparently I am."

Jessica didn't know what to think. She didn't drink, but she knew what it was like to blow up and lash out and pick pieces of other people's skin from beneath her finger-nails. On the other hand, she was getting really, really sick of sharing space with boys who were also capable of blow-ing up and lashing out. She was just so tired of pain. But what she wasn't tired of, and what she was just starting to get a taste of, was honesty. Peter had shared something hard and true with her, and for that she was grateful.

"I'm sorry about your ear," Jessica said.

Peter shrugged. "I deserved it."

"Maybe," Jessica replied, smirking. "Too bad you won't be around for me to teach you how to sing again."

When Jessica came back inside, her dad was sitting at the kitchen table, in the dark, nursing a bottle of Negra Modelo.

"Boys aren't allowed in the house," Rafe said.

Jessica didn't reply. She was too busy humming a little tune to herself.

"There are rules here," Rafe added.

Jessica kept ignoring her father as she made her way back to the staircase. She'd just placed her hand on the banister when Rafe called out her name again. There was something, a pleading sadness in his voice, that made her stop—stop walking, stop humming.

"Anything about that two hundred dollars you were gonna let me borrow?" he asked. "For the truck?"

Jessica should've been mad. Her fingers should've gripped the banister with more force, but she just started up the stairs again and continued to hum.

Iridian
(Sunday, June 16th)

THE ROUTINE ON Sunday was simple. Iridian ate chocolate puffs up on the kitchen counter while Rosa sat in the backyard and tried to talk to the animals. Jessica eventually strolled in wearing her work clothes, but this Sunday she didn't look perfectly perfect. Her hair was thrown up in a clip, and her only makeup was a dash of mascara. She smelled weird, too sharp and sterile, like Lysol or air freshener.

"Dad's asleep in his room," Iridian said.

Jessica grabbed her keys off the kitchen table and left without a word.

Rosa came in just as the Matas' car outside started honking its horn.

"See you later," she said, hustling toward the front door.

Iridian finished her cereal, put the bowl in the dishwater, and then went back to the couch. Once there, she wrote and wrote, page after page after page. She started with another page of *I'm sorry I'm sorry*, but then she tried to write down everything she could remember from her old notebooks upstairs into her new one. She wrote in the margins, in curves around the corners, in between the spiral holes, until her pen started running out of ink.

Eventually, Iridian fell asleep there, with the television on mute and her notebook open on her chest and pen dangling from her fingertips. She woke up a couple of times—once, briefly, when the air conditioner clicked on and she had to pull the blanket up tighter around her shoulders, and again when she heard soft thumps on the stairs and then in the rooms above her head, and she'd assumed that her little sister had come home from church and was trying not to make too much noise.

"Rosa," Iridian croaked. She shifted on the couch so that she was facing the ceiling and watched a spider spin a strand of web between two blades of the unmoving fan. The air conditioner clicked on once more, which was followed by the sound of more footstep-thuds coming from the stairs. The air, Iridian thought, smelled a little like oranges.

Iridian called out her sister's name again, but there was no reply.

"Dad?" she whispered.

Bracing one hand against the side of the couch, Iridian pushed herself to seated, peered toward the staircase, and made a noise—a strained little groan.

Scattered down the staircase were the books—Iridian's books, Ana's books—that had once been stacked neatly in Iridian's closet with their spines facing the wall. They were now spread out, some with their pages yawned open, and some with the pages *missing*, torn out and tossed around. There was paper *everywhere*. The cover of *The Witching Hour* was there, right in Iridian's eyeline. Iridian's notebooks—also once stacked neatly in her closet—were there, too, scattered. Like the books, some were still intact, but just barely. Some were in pieces, ripped—*shredded*. Others were spread open, hanging half on, half off the stairs, like mouths, like big mouths with jaws unhinged from screaming or laughing.

Iridian tumbled off the couch just as she heard someone outside, in the front of the house. There was heavy breathing, grunts, the sound of someone rooting around in the earth by the bushes and bumping against the side of the house.

Rafe, she thought.

It was another bright day, and maybe he was outside doing yard work. That seemed possible. Iridian never ran to her dad in search of safety, but in this instance she didn't know what else to do. She yanked open the front door, pushed against the screen door, and ran out barefoot into the grass.

Rafe wasn't out there doing yard work. What was there was an animal, crouched low on four bent legs. Those legs were black, but its body was spotted, black on tan. A strip of fur all the way down the length of its spine stood taller than the rest. Its dark muzzle was smeared with blood. And there, pinned under one of its front paws, were the remains of a squirrel. The dead animal's bushy tail fluttered in the light breeze, the sunlight shining off its red fur. Iridian watched—still breathless, close to fainting— as that crouched-low animal opened its mouth and its throat started to bob. A sound came out—not a grunt, not breath. A laugh. Hyenas, they laugh like that. They sound like cruel people doubled over and cackling.

Iridian started to shake—not just her hands, but her entire body. The tremors were so violent they caused her teeth to rattle.

"Rosa," she pled feebly.

Rosa did not come, but the animal did. It abandoned the squirrel and stalked forward, its dark eyes pinned on Iridian. It stepped to the side and cut off the path to the front door, as if it somehow knew that Iridian's escape was always inward, never outward.

Iridian looked to the street for help, but she was alone.

"It's fine," she whispered to herself.

It was *not* fine. She was still shaking. The hyena, still laughing, took another step forward, and Iridian let out her own scream. It was a low guttural howl from the back of her raw throat that was like nothing she'd ever produced before.

Again, Iridian looked to the street. Peter Rojas's truck was parked in front of Hector's house, along with a couple other of Hector's friends' cars. The front door to Hector's house was open, but the screen door was closed. All Iridian could think was that she needed to get inside. Inside, anywhere.

The hyena stepped forward, and Iridian took a matching step back. She stepped back again. And again. Light-headed, she gulped, forcing air down into her lungs. The cool grass crunched under her bare feet as she moved— this was good. She just needed to keep moving. She was on the sidewalk and then on the slick asphalt of the street and then on grass again, in Hector's front yard. When she reached the house, she didn't ring the bell, just pulled at the handle. The door was open, and Iridian stumbled inside. Hector's mom was in the living room, sitting on the couch, doing something on her computer with her headphones in.

"Iridian," Mrs. Garcia said, trying to hide her surprise. "Is everything alright?"

Iridian didn't know what to say, so she didn't say anything.

This was a nice house, so different from hers. She'd noticed that when she was here before, last summer. It wasn't dusty. The furniture mostly matched. There was a shelf full of sports-related trophies, and everywhere—on the walls, on side tables—were pictures in frames of Hector and his older sister. They were together, posing and smiling. They were by themselves, posing and smiling. What a nice family.

Iridian flew up the stairs, keeping her gaze on her feet. There was a blade of grass stuck to her big toenail. Pebbles from the road were wedged between her toes.

She could hear the boys even before she reached the top of the stairs. The door to Hector's room was slightly open, and Iridian could see Hector and four of his friends sitting on the floor at the foot of Hector's bed, in front of an old television set. They were passing around a box of cornflakes, scooping out the dry cereal with their hands and shoveling it into their mouths.

Jimmy was closest to the door, so he saw Iridian first, and froze, mid-chew. He nudged Hector, who ignored him. It was only when Iridian pushed open the door fully and stepped into the room that Hector turned his head and saw her.

"Oh . . ." he said. "Uh . . ."

The other boys—Calvin, Luis, and Peter—also turned to face Iridian. They said nothing, just stared.

"There's something outside my house," Iridian choked out. "By the window."

The boys reacted as if they'd suddenly been set on fire. They sprang up, leaping over one another to get to Hector's window. Calvin's hand latched on to the curtains, but he lost his grip when Luis elbowed him in the face. Cornflakes flew from the box, scattering across the bed and floor. Hector tackled Luis, and then tossed him backward. Finally, it was Jimmy who stepped over his pile of friends to reach the window first. He yanked back the curtain and pulled the cord to raise the blinds. He held his breath, looking out and down.

"She's not there," he said. "There's nothing there."

Hector, Luis, and Calvin crowded around him to look.

"There's nothing fucking there, Iridian!" Hector shouted, spinning around. "What the fuck?"

Iridian just stood there, mute and trembling. This was a mistake, a huge mistake. She shouldn't have come here, and she had no idea why Hector was yelling at her.

"Iridian," Peter said.

He was the only one who hadn't wrestled his way across the room. He was standing at the foot of Hector's bed, and the first thing Iridian noticed was how tall he was, taller than Iridian had remembered. He was dressed for work at the pharmacy, wearing a blue collared shirt and khaki pants. There was a small bruise above his eyebrow, and Iridian remembered how Rosa said he'd been in a fight with John.

"Are you okay?" Peter started to reach for Iridian, but thought better of it and withdrew his hand. "What was it? What was there?" He glanced down to Iridian's dirty feet.

"The hyena," she said.

"No way," Hector sneered.

"It was there," Iridian insisted. "In the yard. It was right there."

"There's nothing there," Jimmy whined. Both of his palms were spread out against the glass, and the tip of his nose was squashed flat against the pane.

"I swear it," Iridian said. "I heard something. I thought it was my dad, but when I went to check . . ."

Iridian's voice cracked. What a stupid thing to be doing, crying in a room full of boys she hardly knew, hardly ever spoke to, who she knew thought she was an awkward freak.

"I believe you," Peter replied, turning to face her. "Alright? Just ignore them. They thought it was—"

He paused. Hector, Luis, and Calvin all turned, nearly in unison, away from the window.

"You thought it was *what*?" Iridian asked.

Peter glanced to Hector. "Ana," he said. "We should probably tell you something."

Iridian listened to a story from a year ago about Ana standing outside, tapping on a window, and then Rafe stalking around the yard with a baseball bat. It wasn't the best, most dramatic ghost story she'd ever heard, which is how she knew it was true.

Ana had returned—for her dad, for Iridian and her sisters, for all of them.

"It's true," Iridian said to the boys. "Ana *is* back, but she's not the same anymore."

The Day Iridian Torres Walked Away from the Tenth Grade

IRIDIAN TORRES NEVER went anywhere without three things: a worn-out paperback copy of *The Witching Hour* by Anne Rice, a black-and-white composition notebook, and a peacock blue ink pen. She carried *The Witching Hour* and the notebook with her, from class to class, stacked on top of whatever textbook or binder she was required to have. She always sat in the back row. If there was a window in the room, she'd sit in the desk closest to that. Her spine was always bent way forward, and her legs were folded underneath her on the hard plastic seat. Iridian didn't really talk to people after her sister died, and people didn't really talk to her. But even in mourning, Iridian managed to make pretty good grades, so the teachers gave her a pass when, instead of taking notes, she'd just write in her composition book with her blue ink pen or open up *The Witching Hour* in her lap. Everyone—teachers, other students, staff—figured it was best to leave her alone, not because she would snap at them like Jessica, but because when someone puts up that thick a wall around themselves, you just respect it.

We didn't have uniforms at our school, but Iridian had created her own. She wore white slip-on sneakers, narrow-legged and high-waisted jeans that made her already skinny body appear skinnier, a short-sleeved T-shirt of some kind (always a solid color; never with a graphic), and a jean jacket. The jacket had a patch on it, on the back, over her right shoulder blade. It was of a nopal cactus with a couple of pink flowers in bloom.

We imagined that if some stranger had walked into one of the classrooms and had seen Iridian there, in her uniform, writing in her notebook, they would have thought, *That girl is lost in her own world.* But that wasn't it at all. Iridian wasn't lost, and she was the furthest thing from being in her own world. In truth, Iridian was very aware of the real, *actual* world. The way she sat at her desk, with her long limbs folded up close to her body like an insect— she looked uncomfortable, like everyone else's breath was pressing too hard against her, making her smaller and more compact. She felt everything—*too much*. The world seemed so hard for her to live in.

Of course, we wanted to know what Iridian was writing in her notebooks. Jimmy thought it was some kind of burn book, a list of classmates Iridian felt deserved to suffer the way she clearly suffered. Calvin thought the burn book idea was overdramatic. The answer, according to him, was obvious: Iridian was writing about vampires because Anne Rice wrote about vampires, and if someone reads the exact same book over and over again, it's probably going to get stuck in their brain. That made a lot of sense until Hector pointed out Iridian always carried around *The Witching Hour*, which, by the very title, would seem not to be about vampires, but witches.

We really had no idea what we were talking about, but when we discovered the truth of what Iridian was writing about in her notebooks, it was a nightmare. There weren't any vampires or witches, but it was a nightmare all the same.

On a Tuesday in December, Iridian was in the cafeteria eating lunch alone. Right there, by her tray, like always, was *The Witching Hour*, her composition notebook, and her blue pen. Evalin Uvalde—the girl who was making out with John Chavez until Jessica threw a cup at her face—came up from behind Iridian and snatched her notebook. On instinct, Iridian whipped around and reached back, but Evalin spun out of the way, cackling. Evalin then hopped onto a nearby table and opened Iridian's notebook.

After scanning through a few pages, she landed on one that made her grin so wickedly wide.

This moment was important. It was the moment when the three of us who also had this lunch period, and who were sitting just a couple of tables away from where all this was happening, could've stopped what came next, or *attempted* to stop it and spin its trajectory on a different path. We could've saved Iridian Torres—it was so obvious she needed saving—but we didn't. We remembered what happened the last time we tried saving one of the Torres sisters. Our heroics had backfired in the worst possible way. So instead of doing *anything*, we just sat there, our curiosity burning.

Evalin cleared her throat, and we couldn't help it— we leaned toward the sound. Other students—almost the entire lunchroom—stopped talking and also leaned toward the sound. People hushed each other. Even the workers behind the counters got quieter, or so it seemed. The dings of the registers and the clanks of trays lessened, softened. That day, we were all hungry for nastiness.

"*I have a problem,*" Evalin read out loud, while Iridian curled into herself, shrank deeper into her jean jacket. "*I can write most of the parts, like the parts describing the characters, what they look like, or how it feels when one character wants another character so much their knees turn to jelly and their heart starts to beat all fast and jangled. I know what this feels like. I can write that. But what I can't write are the sex scenes. I have no frame of reference! I've never been with a guy or a girl. I've never even been kissed, and while I'm pretty sure I can fake those descriptions or borrow them from one of Ana's books, that would be . . . disingenuous. I'd feel like a fraud. The descriptions wouldn't be from the heart. It wouldn't be* real, *and I want it to be real."*

Evalin read all this with a fake-earnest tone, and not once did she break character, even though her friends had their hands clasped over their mouths, their eyes watering from holding in their cruel laughter.

It got worse. Of course it did. Evalin looked up from the notebook and straight to where we were sitting.

"I'm thinking about asking one of the boys across the street at Hector's for a favor," she said. *"I wonder if one of them will have sex with me."* Evalin snorted. *"Just once. For research."*

Evalin lost it. She doubled over, gasping and laughing, clutching the notebook to her chest. Her friends all lost it as well. They laughed these loud, full-throated, messy laughs. We could see past the tops of their mouths, to their tongues, to the bits of french fries or the remains of ham sandwiches speckled across those tongues. John Chavez, the biggest shithead in town, was there, hooting and laughing. Eventually, Evalin—still laughing, laughing so hard she was hiccupping—straightened up and put her hand in the air, palm facing forward, silently commanding everyone to wait.

There are two things that gutless boys do when they're being laughed at: They get defensive or they join in. The gazes of the people in the lunchroom that weren't on Iridian—who was still sitting, frozen at her table—were on us. In that moment, we hated Evalin and the evil pride shining in her eyes. We hated watching Iridian fold into herself. Most of all, we hated the fact that we—the ones who had wanted more than anything to be Ana Torres's heroes—buckled under the pressure. We sat there and started laughing, like cowards.

We laughed and laughed at Iridian, but later we talked about how much we hated that we just went along with it. We were sick with regret. It felt like a bunch of slick worms writhing around in our stomachs.

Regret. It's so useless so much of the time.

Evalin wasn't done. She'd needed a moment to compose herself, to shake out her shoulders and take a big breath, like she was some Olympic athlete about to run a big race, before she was able to continue.

She read on: *"I need to know what it feels like, how to do it. I'd like for it to be with someone who doesn't already have a girlfriend and someone who wouldn't feel the need to go tell everyone after it happened, and someone who wasn't a virgin, because it would be helpful if he knew what he was doing. That last thing, the virgin thing, is just a request though, not a requirement. Also, I will not form an attachment."*

Evalin snickered. She looked up from the notebook and tilted her head at us in a gesture of mock sincerity.

"*I promise.*"

There was still laughter throughout the room, but in some corners it had stopped. People with shreds of feeling in their hearts ducked their heads closer to one another, probably whispering about poor Iridian and cruel Evalin. Like us, they didn't do anything but whisper, though. The cash registers went back to their dinging, and the trays went back to their clanging.

One might think Iridian, overcome by embarrassment, would've run from the lunchroom and hid in the bathroom or the library or nurse's office for the rest of the day. She didn't do that. She just sat there, compact, staring straight down at the surface of the table. Her mouth was closed, but her lips were moving, twitching a little, like she was talking to herself.

Iridian's request was for sure a shock, but, when we think about it now, it wasn't totally bizarre. Iridian was the type of girl who was both withdrawn and hyperfocused. She saw things, and not in the dreamy, pseudoclairvoyant way Rosa saw things. Iridian was observant and keen in her own way. She was good with details, sharp like a knife. So it made sense that if she wanted to write something and make it true, she'd really want to *know* the thing she was writing about. She'd want to suck the thing up with her senses and then document it in her notebook.

Finally—*finally*—the bell rang. Iridian grabbed her copy of *The Witching Hour* and snatched her notebook from Evalin's hand, ripping a couple of pages in the process, and left the lunchroom. That was the last day we ever saw her at school.

Rosa

(Sunday, June 16th)

"IT CAME FOR you?"

Rosa was crouched in front of a bush in the yard, examining a bit of loose squirrel fur the color of red clay. At the same time, she was fighting down the strange urge to cause petty harm to her sister. It was like she wanted to tug out a strand of Iridian's hair or step down on her bare big toe. Rosa had never felt that way before.

"It didn't come *for* me," Iridian explained. "It was just here."

"How did it seem?" Rosa urged. "Like, how did it look? Was it sick?"

Iridian obviously didn't know how to respond to that, so Rosa's focus shifted from the fur tangled in the bushes over to Hector's house, where a jumble of boy-shaped shadows had appeared at the upper window. A bird cawed from a nearby tree.

"Come on," Rosa said, standing. "It's getting dark. Let's go inside."

"Wait." Iridian latched on to Rosa's arm, a little too hard. "Did you not hear what I told you, about the boys, about Ana? They said—"

"I know what they said," Rosa replied. "They told you about how they saw her ghost by the window last summer. I know. They sent me a note when it happened."

When Rosa looked into her sister's eyes, she saw a hunger there. Or like a *dis*-ease, a wildness. Maybe that wildness had passed to Iridian from the hyena. Iridian squeezed Rosa's arm harder, and Rosa's urge to tug a piece of Iridian's hair got stronger.

Everything was connected.

Rosa was on the bus on the way back to San Fernando. It wasn't the first time she'd been to church twice on the same Sunday, but there was a new kind of urgency to this trip. She supposed she could have tried to find Walter's mom for a ride—Walter was probably still at church, working—but she wanted to be alone before talking to Father Mendoza.

Sunday buses were usually empty, and Rosa's bus was no exception. It was just her, a woman in a uniform—a knee-length pink dress and tan-colored tights that made her seem like she worked in a diner—and the driver. Traffic was light, and the bus was only a couple of stops away from the church when the driver slammed on his brakes. Rosa flew—forehead first—into the seat in front of her. Dazed, she checked for blood, but there was no cut, just a tender spot that would for sure form a goose egg. The woman in the pink dress, though, was moaning from the floor. She'd been thrown completely out of her seat and was in a crumpled heap, bleeding from the mouth. There was a long run in her tights, all the way up her shin.

The driver got to the woman before Rosa could. He was trying to open a first aid kit and speak into his radio at the same time. He was saying something about an animal running out into the street, and how he'd had to come to a sudden stop to avoid hitting it.

"It looked sort of like a dog," he said. "Or like a real skinny wolf."

Rosa bolted out the side doors of the bus, first checking under the wheels and then looking frantically up and down the street. She thought she saw something—a flicker of a shadow low to the ground—on the other side of a parked car, and she ran toward it. There was nothing there, but then that same flicker caught her eye, this time as if it had just rounded the corner of a building up ahead. It was leading her closer and closer to the church.

This was perfect. This was just what she'd been hoping for.

Like last time, there was a line of people waiting to see Father Mendoza, but Rosa shoved ahead of all of them.

"I have another question," Rosa said, standing across from the priest's desk.

Father Mendoza's dry-kindling eyes were, as usual, patient and kind. His stark white office wasn't the type of room that Rosa expected would change much from day to day, but she hadn't expected it to be exactly the same as before. There were the same simple cross, the same simple ticking clock, and also the same line of ants marching in the same curve up the wall behind where the priest sat.

"Is it possible," she began, still slightly out of breath, "for the spirit of a person to enter another creature?"

"You're talking about possession?" Father Mendoza asked. "Like when a demon enters a person's body?"

"Not a demon, no. I'm wondering if the spirit of a person can enter the body of an animal." Rosa paused to look to the ants on the white wall. "Or an insect."

"Is that what you think has happened with Ana?" Father Mendoza asked.

"Yes," Rosa replied. "Maybe, yes. There were fireflies and a bird that fell. And the hyena. It escaped from the zoo on the anniversary of the day my sister died. It killed a squirrel on our front lawn." There was a little pinch in

Rosa's heart, and she pushed the palm of her hand against her chest. "I think . . . it may be close by."

Father Mendoza was quiet for a moment. Then he asked, "You think your sister is controlling these things?"

"Yes," Rosa replied. "Does this mean something?"

For a long time, Father Mendoza said nothing. He had to have known there was still a line of people waiting outside to speak with him, but he didn't look at his ticking clock. Rosa could see a spark in his eyes, like he was calling to mind a memory. He was off somewhere, in the room but not in the room. Rosa knew what that was like.

"Ever since you came last time, I've been doing some thinking," he finally said, "and I have a question of my own. Why is it Ana who is doing these things? Why isn't it your mother?"

Rosa suddenly felt very heavy. Over the course of the last year, she and her priest had talked for hours and hours about faith and death and the meaning of life, but they'd never talked about Rosa's mother. Rita de la Cruz was a woman who had grown up in the Rio Grande Valley, who'd met Rafe Torres when they'd both been in the ninth grade, and who'd died just hours after giving birth to Rosa. All Rosa knew was that, during the delivery, something had gone wrong. There was blood loss. Even the strongest heart can't beat without blood.

"I've never told you this," Father Mendoza went on, "but I knew Rita. I'm a couple of years younger than her, but we both grew up in Mission. It's a small place. Everyone knew everyone."

Father Mendoza's chair squeaked as he sat back and brought his fingers into a tent. His eyes were doing what dry kindling does when it heats up. They were smoldering. Rosa knew what was coming. Her priest was about to launch into a story. He probably thought this story, which would no doubt be about the young Rita de la Cruz down in Mission, Texas, was going to be a gift Rosa could then take home with her and cherish like a bird's bright feather or a perfectly coiled snail shell. Father Mendoza probably thought he was being kind and generous. But Rosa knew his story wouldn't really have anything to do with Rosa *or* her mother. She could tell by the warm glow in his eyes that, even if the story seemed on the surface to be about Rita de la Cruz, it was really about him.

"Our mothers had been friends since high school," he said, "but it wasn't until Rita was fifteen that we officially met. I was thirteen."

Rosa looked to the cross on the wall, and then to the clock. She closed her eyes and took a breath. Father Mendoza wasn't *listening*. She'd come to him with something specific and important, and he was turning it into something about himself. He was launching into this tale as if he had all the time in the world to tell it, as if it wasn't getting late in the day or if there wasn't a small mob of people still waiting outside his door for his counsel.

"You look a lot like her," Father Mendoza said.

Rosa felt even heavier. What a waste this was turning out to be. Jessica had always had a bad taste in her mouth when it came to priests, and now Rosa was beginning to understand why.

Just a moment earlier, Father Mendoza had said, "Everyone knew everyone." Rosa disagreed. No one knew anyone. Not really.

She wasn't there to argue that point, though, so she put up her hand, palm facing out, just like she'd seen Father Mendoza do hundreds of times while he led services. He'd hold one hand like that while the other rested on the opened pages of a Bible. The priest saw Rosa's hand, and he stopped talking.

"Thank you," Rosa said. "I'm leaving now."

Rosa found Walter outside, sweeping the steps. He was facing away from her and didn't know she was there. Rosa liked the look of it: Walter, a tall boy with strong arms, sweeping stone in the twilight. Still unaware of Rosa, Walter stopped his work and looked for a moment to the darkening sky, to the lightning flashes in the distance. She liked the look of that, too: a boy watching a storm.

"Walter!" Rosa called out.

Walter turned. "Everything alright?" he asked.

"After I figure all this out," Rosa said, approaching him, "about Ana, I'd like to go with you to the basement and abandoned rooms of the church."

"Okay." Walter laughed. "Of course."

Rosa reached for Walter's hand, and Walter let her take it. She didn't thread her sweat-damp fingers with his, but she held his right hand, palm up, in her left hand. Then she touched it. For what felt like a long time, she traced Walter's fingers across his rough fingertips and the blunt edge of each of his nails. She pictured these fingers holding hammers and light bulbs and ladder rungs. She pressed her thumb into the mound under his thumb. She spread his fingers wide to feel the webbing between them. This was a hand that did things. Rosa liked that. She liked that he wasn't a ghost, or a phantom animal. If she wanted, she could walk up to him and touch him.

Jessica

(early Monday, June 17th)

JESSICA AND JOHN had spent the last ten hours together, and she'd been half there for all of them. After her shift, she had gone to John's house because he'd told her to come to his house. They'd watched television. They'd driven around. They'd gotten burgers from a drive-through. They'd parked and eaten those burgers in the car and then made out a little even though John's mouth tasted like meat and Jessica wasn't really into it. Then they'd driven around some more. They'd talked. Well, John had talked. He'd talked about how his older cousin was never home anymore now that he'd enrolled in some classes at the community college, and because of that, John had to do more chores around the house. He may have talked about some other stuff, but

Jessica hadn't really been listening. For sure, she hadn't said anything back. He'd never asked her anything about herself or her job or her family. Eventually, Jessica pulled up outside her house, thinking that John would get the point. He didn't. The engine was off. The windows were rolled down. It was nearly five in the morning, and Jessica was so very over all of this. She thought back to when she was in grade school, in the choir. Her heart used to feel so full.

Jessica had a song stuck in her head, one she'd heard at work that day, probably seven or eight times. John was still talking as she looked out the windows and started humming to herself.

"Jess?" John urged. "What are you doing?"

Jessica closed her eyes and kept right on humming.

"Jess!" John grabbed Jessica's arm and shook her a little.

Jessica turned to hum in John's face, so close and so sloppy, spit flung from her lips to his. John blinked and leaned back.

"You've changed," he said.

The bruises around John's eye were still black and plum-colored, ringed with mucus yellow. It was sort of a masterpiece.

"You're making excuses to not see me," he added. "And you're acting all mean."

"That's not true," Jessica replied half-heartedly.

"It *is* true."

"Do you want me to take you home?" Jessica asked.

John said nothing. It was hard for Jessica to take him seriously, with his eye looking like that. She bit back a smile.

"So," she said, "I guess you just want to sit here and do nothing?"

"Fuck!" John shouted. Jessica recoiled and John leaned forward to press the tip of his nose into her ear. This time she felt *his* spit on *her* skin. *"Fuck!"*

"Stop," Jessica gasped.

"You stop!" John yelled.

"I'll just take you home." Jessica tried to twist her key in the ignition, but John stopped her.

"You're not listening to me! What's wrong with you?"

"Are you serious?" Jessica spun in her seat. "Are you *just* now realizing that something is wrong with me?"

Jessica opened her car door, but John reached across her and slammed it back shut. She grabbed frantically for her phone to call her sisters inside, but John snatched it from her hand and tossed it out his window and into the grass. He did the same thing with her car keys: yanked them out of the ignition and tossed them out the window. Then he took both of her arms, pinned them to her sides, and pressed his forehead against her temple. Jessica's whole spine rattled, and a scream rose up, which John cut off by pulling her forward then slamming her back against the seat. Her head bounced against the headrest, and for a second, Jessica saw stars.

"I worry about you," he grunted. "I'm worried you don't know how much I love you."

Jessica felt sick, but there was a little voice inside her chanting: fight, *fight*. She didn't know how to win a fight with John, though. She needed to think. She needed to buy some time.

"If you're quiet, I can sneak you up to my room," she offered. "Then I can take you home before I have to go to work."

"You're *not listening*." John pressed against her, skull to skull now. "Have you ever been scared, Jessica?"

What was John talking about? What *the fuck* did he know about being scared? How dare he ask her that, as if he knew the first thing about fear, about the blinding claustrophobia that went along with being trapped in a car, in a house, with a ghost, with a living person?

The worst fear of all, Jessica was coming to realize, was the fear of having no idea who she was. Jessica had become a ghost, and not a good kind of ghost like Ana or like the ones that maybe haunted centuries-old churches. She was acting like a small spirit. She was so mad all the time, but instead of striking out, she would do nothing or reach out with tentative, tissue-paper fingers. She had to do better. An angry girl was allowed to be angry. Earlier that day, in the pharmacy, Jessica had watched a girl her age screaming at her boyfriend in the allergy medicine aisle. The girl had kept yelling, "When were you going to tell me? When were you going to tell me, huh?" The boy kept trying to calm her down, but she wouldn't have it. Eventually, Mathilda came out with a security guard, and the girl had yelled, "Fuck this!" and then thrown a bottle of nasal spray at the boy's head.

Jessica had been transfixed. The scene had been so *inspiring*. Jessica had to start. She had to start scraping away the layers. This—this shit with John—was the first step, and, if she was honest with herself, it was the easiest because John was a total fucking loser.

"Get out of my car," Jessica said.

"Did you not hear me?" John asked. His disgusting meat breath poured into Jessica's ear, and she couldn't help it: She laughed. Then she pried one of her hands free and smashed down on her horn.

John was startled enough to allow Jessica to reach for her door handle again, but before she could fully open it, he grabbed her arms again, squeezing tighter. This time, it didn't matter that Jessica didn't know how to win. She fought anyway.

"Get out!" Jessica screamed, flailing against him. *"Get out!"*

She repeated those two words over and over again at the top of her lungs. The words stopped being words and became shrieks. Jessica stared straight into John's bruised eyes and continued to scream. For the first time, she wanted the whole neighborhood to be her witness.

Iridian

(early Monday, June 17th)

GIVEN THAT HER name meant "relating to the eye," it was ironic how selective Iridian's vision was. The things she wanted to see mostly lived in her head or in the worlds she created on paper. She could picture a character's skin in such vivid detail, she knew how it tasted. She knew so clearly—in her mind—the difference between eyes that sparkled with tears and those that sparkled with joy and those that sparkled with pride. The things she didn't want to see, she avoided. Instead of burying her head in the sand, she buried herself between book pages or under bedsheets or, now, into couch cushions. Rosa knew her sister well, so she'd known the solution to Ana's writing on the wall was to cover it up. She'd also known that the solution to Ana's destroying Iridian's books and notebooks was to simply pick everything up and put it back into the closet.

Iridian's new notebook was snug against her side, and the television was still on soap operas, still on mute. She wished she lived there—in the screen, in the beautiful houses on the screen where people spoke but you couldn't hear their muted words. At some point, Iridian fell asleep to that beauty. She woke when a lamp clicked on—more like, she jerked awake. Her long legs bucked against the tangle of her blanket. Iridian blinked and saw her father at the far end of the couch. With a dried crust of spittle at the edge of his mouth, he was the opposite of the beauty on the screen.

"What?" Iridian asked.

Rafe said nothing. A little knowing twitch played at the corner of his mouth, right next to the spit.

Iridian looked down and, there, clutched in her father's hand, was her notebook, the new one with the yellow cover. She exhaled hard and fast, and before she could even really think about it, Iridian launched off the couch. She collided with Rafe, and her notebook flipped open, its ink-covered pages fanning out. Iridian's nails dug into the skin of Rafe's wrist and the backs of his hands. Her attack worked—sort of. Rafe pulled away, but all Iridian was left with was a tiny scrap of paper with the word *ravage* written on it.

"This is what you think about?" Rafe demanded. "What kind of girl are you?"

"It's nothing," Iridian lied, because it was, of course, everything.

"It's filth! It's *trash*!"

Rafe waited for his daughter to respond, maybe to apologize, and Iridian waited for Rafe to do what he always did: say something terrible and then try to twist things to make it seem as if Iridian had been the one to force *him* into saying something terrible.

Rafe took a step forward, and, out of the corner of her eye, Iridian saw Rosa creep down the stairs. Iridian steeled her nerves, took a breath, and remembered how diligently she had practiced for this sort of thing. It was rare he could hurl an insult at her that she hadn't hurled at herself already.

"I know why you do this," Rafe said. "You're trying to make up for the fact that you aren't beautiful like Ana, talented like Jessica, or kind like Rosa. You are just . . ." He paused, trying to find the right words. "You are a nothing person. Not beautiful. Not talented. Not kind. I thought I raised you better, but I guess I was wrong."

Before, when this had happened at school, when her secrets had been plucked away and shared by and to her awful classmates, Iridian had been so humiliated she hadn't been able to move. She'd heard the jeers and laughter, but only over the white-noise roar in her head.

For a long, long time, Iridian had wanted to be completely inconspicuous, homebound, so introverted she was practically invisible. But *nothing*? Iridian didn't want to be nothing, and when she heard her father say that to her, she exploded like a star.

With a sharp cry, she lunged for the notebook again, but Rafe held it above his head, toward the overhead light and out of his daughter's reach. Iridian tried to claw her way up his arm, but Rafe pushed her hard—right in the center of her chest—and she fell back against the couch and then bounced onto the floor. Rafe started to flip through the pages, just like Evalin had done, like he was going to read from them. She couldn't bear the thought of her words coming out of his mouth, so she screamed. Still on the floor, she folded herself into the tiniest ball possible, closed her eyes, covered her ears with her hands, and screamed.

Rafe started reading. Iridian couldn't hear everything, but the worst/best phrases seemed to rise over her screams: *suck, smack, salty.* She screamed louder. Eventually, Rafe grabbed her by the arm and tried to pull her up, but Iridian was dead weight, a shrieking heap. Rafe was dragging her across the carpet. Her shoulder twisted, threatening to wrench out of joint, but Iridian kept screaming. She vaguely heard Rosa telling Rafe to let go, but Rafe wasn't listening. He bent over Iridian and told her—*shouted*—into her ear, "If only your mother—God rest her precious soul—could see this."

"*Stop!*" Rosa yelled.

Iridian was able to turn her head and see that her sister had pulled a nearby lamp from its electrical socket. She held that lamp in both her hands, wielding it like a baseball bat. Its cord dangled to the ground.

Outside, someone honked the horn of their car.

Then, Iridian felt something unmistakable: wind.

It was warm, and it was so strong that it blew back the loose strands of her hair. Iridian had to tilt her face away to protect it from the grit she felt flying into her eyes, but there was nothing she could do to avoid the smell of oranges that the wind carried with it.

In the next instant, the television blinked off. A high, whining sound came from its screen, and Iridian watched as the glass shattered on its own, radiant, as if a fist had been slammed in the center of it.

"Leave, Iridian," Rosa commanded, tightening her grip on the lamp. She was focused on Rafe. "Go outside. I'll take care of this."

Once outside, Iridian heard Jessica shrieking from her car. Through the open passenger-side window, she saw her sister thrashing against her seat, and John was trying to keep her pinned down. A different kind of wind blew through—rain was coming—but a piece of Iridian's hair got stuck in her mouth, and she could taste the dry dust. She thought of Rosa, always swooping in to save her, as she'd just done seconds ago with Rafe. She could still hear the both of them, behind her, yelling at each other in the house. Rafe was yelling, "This is my house!" but Iridian knew that wasn't true anymore. Her father had no control over what was happening in those walls.

Iridian ran toward Jessica's car—toward Jessica's shrieking. She was determined to be the hero for once. She was fed up with men trying to leave their bruises all over her and her sisters.

Jessica

(early Monday, June 17th)

THE PASSENGER DOOR opened, and John was being yanked from the car. Jessica could see Iridian behind him, her arms around him, tugging him backward. John quickly found his feet, however, then spun around and backhanded Iridian across the face. She fell hard against the side of the car, her head whacking the metal frame, and then crumpled to the curb.

All the air left Jessica's body. She couldn't have possibly seen what she'd seen. She blinked, and there was Iridian, on the ground, grimacing, her hand coming up to press against her temple and her thigh scraped from where she'd skidded against the concrete.

Jessica was out of the car, stalking John around the

front end. There was a sound in her head, like a pulse, like a *whomp, whomp, whomp.* Pressure was building behind her ears, in the palms of her hands. She was about to explode.

"I will fucking kill you," she said to John, her voice hoarse. "You hit my sister, and I will *fucking* kill you."

Jessica shoved John in the chest with both hands, but all he did was stumble, laugh, then spit on the street. Too fast, John reached out and grabbed a chunk of Jessica's hair, right at the root. She yelped as he gripped her hair tighter and attempted to push her back into her car.

Jessica's eyes watered from the sudden burst of pain, but she could still recognize the blur of red fabric that had suddenly appeared in her vision. Rosa was there, swinging some kind of weapon at him. After the sickening thud of metal on meat, there was a noise, a grunt. John fell away, yanking out strands of Jessica's hair. Again, Rosa brought her weapon up over her head and swung it at the soft part of John's side, right under his ribs. This time, John bellowed, gripped his torso, and landed hard on one knee.

Jessica heard the bang of a storm door, then another. She looked around and saw her wish from before had come true. Her neighbors were out of their houses. Mrs. Moreno from next door was on her front porch in her bathrobe, yelling into her cell phone and gesturing wildly with her free hand. Teddy Arenas was out in the driveway, cradling his little dog. Mrs. Bolander was at the front edge of her yard in a matching pajama set—pink with watermelons.

Hector and his friends were there. They were out of breath, like they'd just sprinted down the stairs. Peter wasn't with them. He must've been at the pharmacy.

At last, Jessica turned to her own house and saw her father, standing in the open doorway clutching paper in his hand. He hadn't come out to help—he never, ever helped them.

Rosa was still gripping her weapon—a lamp without its shade, Jessica now realized. Its cord dragged across the patchy grass. Rafe slumped against the doorframe, placing his hand over his heart, and that's when Jessica noticed he was wearing one of Ana's old bracelets on his wrist. It was made out of yellow string and a couple of beads. Where on earth had he found that?

It had just been a little over a week ago that Rafe had been in the middle of the street, bruised and crying out, needing help. Jessica had rushed to his side. She'd stopped her car in the middle of the road and had thrown herself at her father. And this is what she got in return, when she was the one who needed help—nothing.

Jessica could see, at the edge of her vision, her neighbors taking slow steps closer to her house, to her yard, to her and her sisters. She remembered, half-remembered, the night that Ana died. It was sticky out—just like now. Rafe was slumped in the doorway—just like now. Jessica and her sisters had needed help, and the neighbors had come rushing from their houses. She remembered screaming against a woman's body. She still didn't know whose. She just remembered the woman's shirt smelled a little bit sour-sweet, like red wine.

"We're leaving," Rosa said to her sisters, dropping the lamp in the grass. She bent to pick up Jessica's phone and keys from where John had pitched them in the yard, and climbed into the passenger seat. "Iridian, are you all right?"

"I'm fine," Iridian muttered. She hauled herself to standing.

"In the car, then," Rosa commanded. "Now."

Iridian did as she was told. Jessica started the engine, and Rosa leaned out the passenger window.

"John, hey," she called out.

John scowled up at Rosa. It was the scowl of a wounded animal. He had his hand pressed against his side. Jessica knew there would be a bruise there. She wanted his whole body covered in bruises.

"You broke my ribs, you little bitch!" John spit out.

"Good," Rosa said. "And if I ever see you on this street again, I will break your spine."

Iridian

(early Monday, June 17th)

WHEN IRIDIAN'S HEAD had hit the side of her sister's car, she'd accidentally bitten down on her tongue. There'd been a gush of hot blood, so sudden Iridian had nearly choked. She'd turned her ringing head and spit bloody gobs onto the curb. Now, as she sat in the back seat of Jessica's car, her tongue was swollen and tender, still bleeding. She had nowhere to spit, so every so often, she was forced to swallow a mouthful of blood. Somehow those mouthfuls of blood went down easier than when her dad had called her a "nothing person."

Of all the insults Iridian had hurled at herself in her bathroom mirror, she'd never thought of calling herself "nothing." It was the worst insult of all—worse than being called ugly or miserable or bird-thin or stupid. It was as if Rafe had taken a hot metal spoon and cleanly scooped out her insides. She'd been left feeling hollow and hungry.

Then, when the TV screen had shattered and Rosa had come to her rescue, Iridian hadn't felt relief. Or fear. She had cried out in desperation and grabbed for paper as if paper could save her life. Rosa had told her to leave and go outside, and Iridian had the time for one last attempt. Rafe had been disoriented, and Iridian had leapt forward. Her fingers had closed around a page from her notebook. There'd been ripping—holes being torn from the metal spiral. She'd been left with a shred, less than half a page. She'd held on to that shred as she'd bolted outside. She'd still held on to that scrap of paper as John's knuckles had crashed into her cheekbone and her head had chimed with the impact.

That scrap of paper was still wadded up in Iridian's sweaty fist, where it was safe, and where no one else could reach it.

Jessica's phone rattled gently in the cup holder in the center console. It had been doing that off and on since they'd left the house.

"You should have left it in the yard," Jessica told Rosa.

Iridian clenched her fist tighter and looked out to the flashing night sky. Cool winds buffeted the car. Jessica's windows were rolled down like they always were, and little leaves were blowing into the cabin. They would come in one window, spin in a tiny roller-coaster loop-de-loop, and then go out the opposite window. Jessica's car had always been as much of a mess as her room, so bits of trash—plastic straw wrappers and old receipts—were flying around in loops as well. Outside there was a storm coming, and inside it was a mini-cyclone. It had rained so much over the course of the last week, Iridian half hoped that by the time she and her sisters returned to their house, there would be no house, or that maybe just the peaks of the roof would be visible. She imagined the soft, rain-soaked ground swallowing the wood and the bricks, sucking it all down with a burp.

"I'm not sorry." Rosa turned toward Jessica and tried with little success to tuck the long strands of her hair behind her ears.

"I know," Jessica replied. "I just wish I were the one who had done it. Everyone's been fighting my battles lately." She paused and looked to Iridian in the rearview mirror. "What happened at the house?"

"He found my stories," Iridian said. "He read them. He wouldn't give them back."

"Then Ana got mad," Rosa said, smirking. "She broke the TV."

"Did you know about John?" Iridian blurted. She met her sister's sharp glance in the rearview mirror.

"Did I know *what* about John?" Jessica asked.

"How he drove off." Iridian paused to nibble on the inside of her lip, where the skin had split and blood was still trickling out. "After seeing Ana slip, he left her there in the yard."

Jessica's eyes slid back down to the road. "Who told you that?"

"Peter," Iridian replied. "He said he and his friends had watched it all from the window."

"That's not what he told me," Jessica said. "He said they didn't see the car. And when were you talking to Peter Rojas?"

"I was at Hector's," Iridian replied.

She then told her sister about what had happened with her notebooks, the smell of oranges, and the hyena.

Fat drops started to fall on the windshield, and Jessica turned on the wipers. Several seconds passed, and the only sound was the *click-swish* of the blades skimming across the glass.

"What else did *Peter* say?" she urged.

Rosa shifted in the passenger seat.

"He said he and his friends saw Ana's ghost," Iridian replied. "Last summer. She was outside, tapping on Dad's window. Rosa knows."

"They left me a note," Rosa said.

Jessica's expression was unreadable, which meant she was furious—because maybe she'd learned the truth about John and Ana, but also because the boys had seen the ghost and had thought to tell Rosa and not her. Jessica had always believed that Ana belonged to her and only her. There'd been the insistence on moving into her room and smoking her cigarettes, but Iridian knew Jessica had also spent the weeks immediately following Ana's death building shrines. She refused to throw anything of Ana's away, and would pile up used mascara tubes and hair ties and half-eaten boxes of SweeTarts all over the floor. They were tiny ofrendas, built there as if to welcome Ana back, as if she'd just momentarily lost her way out the window that night. So, no. Jessica wouldn't have liked hearing that Ana had appeared to the boys across the street—and not her—an entire year ago.

"Where are we going?" Rosa asked.

Good question. Iridian had been so stunned by everything that had just happened, she'd failed to realize they were driving farther and farther away from her house, her street, her neighborhood. She started to panic a little. She didn't know how far the chain on her anchor would stretch before it snapped.

"To the pharmacy," Jessica said. "Iridian's bleeding. She needs stuff."

Again, Iridian tongued the wound in her mouth. Then she tapped her fingertips up her thigh. The skin there was pricked and torn. It burned when she touched it, so yes, she guessed she needed *stuff*.

"You two can just wait in the car if you want," Jessica said. "Let me know if you can think of anything you need—anything for the house."

"I need a new notebook," Iridian said. "And another pen."

Jessica

(early Monday, June 17th)

FOR THE LAST year, Jessica had heard all kinds of things because most people didn't have the decency to wait until she was out of earshot before they ran their mouths. They'd accused Jessica of being desperate. They'd wondered what she could have possibly been thinking. Of course, she'd known John and Ana had been seeing each other for months up until the time Ana died. That was the reason she'd pursued John in the first place. Jessica coped with her sister's death by *becoming* her sister. She'd wanted Ana's room, her clothes, her makeup, her boyfriend. Looking back, that all seemed so stupid. Maybe not stupid. Maybe more like grief-sick. Now all this time had passed, and Jessica was still stuck hard in the role as Ana-Not-Ana-Not-Jessica.

And then there was Peter. *Fucking* Peter. Peter got everything, and Jessica got nothing. Peter got to see Ana knocking on a window at night. All Jessica got was a shadowed hand and wicked laugh. Peter got the glory of fighting John and winning. Peter got to take a quick trip to Mexico and then wash his hands of Southtown.

As she pulled her car into the parking lot of the pharmacy, Jessica itched at her scalp, then between each of her fingers. She wished she could scratch off all of her skin and start over.

With her sisters waiting in the car, Jessica stalked across the parking lot. Before she'd even made it through the pharmacy's doors, her phone chimed once, then again. She tugged it out of her pocket and chucked it into a trash can.

Cotton squares, hydrogen peroxide, a tube of Neosporin. She'd just bought these things for John, and here she was, buying them again for Iridian, who had gone outside twice in two days and had been damaged each time because of it.

When Jessica turned into the school supply aisle to grab a pen and another notebook, there was Peter, just a few feet away, bent over and hacking at a taped-up box with a cutter. She knew that blade. The handle was cracked and held together with bright blue duct tape.

"I used that box cutter on Evalin Uvalde's tires," Jessica said.

"Everyone knew it was you," Peter replied, with a glance over his shoulder. He said it like it was no big revelation, like it was no surprise Jessica was a petty vandal. "No one could prove it, though."

"I should've slashed your tires, too," Jessica added.

Peter's blade stilled. He sat back on his heels.

"Are you fighting with me again?" He looked to the basket in Jessica's hand and rose to his feet. "What happened?"

Jessica still itched like she wanted to peel off her skin, and now the spot on her head where John had grabbed her hair started to throb. She was so tired of boys pulling on her, attempting to invade the life she'd tried so hard to keep protected.

Again, Peter eyed the contents of Jessica's basket and then did a quick scan of her body: her bare legs, her wrists, her throat, her face. As he breathed out, his lips separated slightly. He was concerned. Jessica didn't want him to look at her like that. She wanted him to look at her like that. *She* wanted to look at *him* like that. She had no idea.

Jessica needed a foothold. She needed to feel strong again, and the only way she knew how to do that was to make someone else feel weak.

"Did you know?" Jessica began. "Did you know that a couple of months ago, I actually managed to get Iridian out of the house? We went to the mall. For a while, it went okay. We walked around, went into a couple stores. But when we stopped at the food court for sodas, Iridian froze. She thought she'd seen someone from school. It turned out it wasn't who she thought it was, but still. She refused to move. She just sat there. At one of the tables, for hours. *Hours*."

"What happened?" Peter repeated. "Jessica, what's going on?"

"I sat there with her," Jessica continued, "until the mall was closing and all the people were leaving, and I was finally able to convince her to walk with me to the car. That is the kind of sister I have." She paused. "*You* did that to her."

Peter held Jessica's gaze. "You're right. I didn't say anything. I could've helped her, but I laughed like an idiot. I'm sorry."

"Have you told *her* you're sorry?" Jessica urged. "The other day, maybe? When she was over at Hector's house?"

Jessica was so, so angry. It wasn't just about John and the pain he'd left behind. She was angry that the ghost of her older sister was playing tricks on her and her sisters and that Iridian had been quasi-hunted in their front yard by a zoo animal gone feral, but she was also angry—more than she could ever describe—that Iridian had gone across the street and sought help from the boys who'd proven over and over again they were no help at all—that they were, instead, meddling little shit cowards.

"No," Peter replied. "I did not."

"Of course you didn't," Jessica scoffed. "But I bet you asked what you could do to help. Since you're so fucking helpful."

Peter tried to say something, but Jessica cut him off.

"What happened in the lunchroom wouldn't have ever happened if you and your friends hadn't decided to *help* us last summer." Her voice was rising. "Iridian doesn't need your *help*. *I* don't need your help. We'll never need your fucking help, Peter. It is *not* your business what happens in *my* house, to *my* family."

"Okay," Peter insisted. He paused. "Jessica, what is this about? Are you okay?"

Jessica cackled, full-throated. "You can't have her! Ana's *my* sister. You can't have her!"

"I-I . . ." Peter stammered. "Jessica. It's not . . ."

"She's *my* sister!" Jessica slapped a hand to her chest. "And *you* saw her! You saw her, right? Her whole body, from head to toe, out in front of the window?"

Peter nodded.

"I've seen her *hand*," Jessica said. "And I've heard her laugh. Just once. That's it. Why is that? Why would she come to you and not to me? How is that fair? How is that fucking fair, huh?"

The movement was slight, but Peter's gaze caught on something over Jessica's shoulder. Jessica turned and saw Mathilda standing in the aisle, looking alarmed.

"Everything okay here?" Mathilda asked.

"Fine," Peter replied.

"I heard about what happened to your sister." Mathilda gave Jessica a sympathetic smile. "It was this time last year, wasn't it?"

Jessica bit the inside of her cheek to keep from screaming. Everyone, *everyone* knew everything. Everyone had pieces of Ana, and no one deserved them.

Jessica felt Peter's arms around her—not around her like to bring her into an embrace, but to steer her away from Mathilda and through the back door into the stockroom. Jessica wanted an embrace, though. She wanted one so badly. She swiveled toward Peter, colliding with him. She pressed her forehead into his shirt and sobbed. Then she pressed her lips against his shirt. She felt his heartbeat, beneath the fabric, beneath his skin. Peter didn't belong to her, Jessica knew, but in that moment, she was claiming him. She had never done anything so wonderful as kiss Peter's shirt. She pushed and pushed against him, but he didn't waver.

Even as she pushed against him, she was saying, "Please, just leave me alone."

Peter didn't let her go, though, and she didn't let him go, either.

Iridian

(early Monday, June 17th)

"WHAT ARE YOU holding?" Rosa had shifted in her seat and was looking at the wisp of paper edging out from Iridian's fist. There was static in the pre-storm air, causing the strands of Rosa's hair to lift and stick to the headrest.

"Is it from your notebook? Were you able to save something?"

Yes. It *did* feel like Iridian had saved something. It felt like she was keeping something alive and warm, egglike, in the palm of her hand.

"Read it," Rosa said. "I'd like to hear it."

Iridian said nothing. Outside, a bright ragged line cut across the sky, and the corresponding boom of thunder made Iridian's head throb.

"Please," Rosa urged.

Iridian looked to her sister, her kind sister, who was waiting patiently—as if Rosa would wait any other way. Her static-puffed hair was a brown halo. Rosa had captured the energy of the oncoming storm, sucked it inside her, and made it beautiful. Just minutes ago, Rosa had attacked John, and possibly Rafe before that. That had also been beautiful.

When Iridian glanced down at her fist, she again saw the long, angry scrapes on her leg, extending from her knee up to the middle of her thigh. The blood was dry, but the scrapes still stung. The hurt was deeper than it looked. She'd been struck by a boy, and she'd never forget it. Her stomach hurt. Her head hurt. It beat like a heavy heart. Her tongue hurt. It was swollen and, if she read out loud what was on the paper, her words would maybe sound funny.

"I was jealous," Rosa said.

Iridian looked to her sister, confused.

"When you told me about the hyena," Rosa clarified. "I was upset that you saw it and I didn't. I didn't know what I was feeling because I don't think I've ever felt it before. I was mad at you and wanted to pull your hair. I'm sorry. I don't feel that way anymore, by the way."

"Oh," Iridian said. "Okay."

"Will you please now read what you have?"

Iridian loosened her fist a fraction, then all the way.

The paper was wadded and damp from her sweat, but in the glow given off by the lights in the parking lot, she could still make out her handwriting—chicken scratches, an ugly mash-up of print and cursive she'd attempted to make beautiful with bright blue ink. She hadn't even looked at what was on the paper until now. She could've torn anything from her father's grasp. It could've been a long description of how a tongue feels against another tongue or a series of incomplete sentences. It could've been blank.

It wasn't blank. Or about tongues.

On one side there was a cut-off sentence that started with *I want*, but then after that, *I'm sorry I'm sorry I'm sorry* was written at least ten times.

Iridian passed the paper up to Rosa and then told her the story—about finding the pregnancy test, about turning Ana's crisis into *her* crisis, about calling her favorite sister a dumb whore. She could barely get those last words out. She hadn't said them for a year, since saying them to Ana.

"I tried to tell her I was sorry, like right then," Iridian said, "but she wouldn't accept it. She told me I'd fucked up. Sometimes it's all I can think about."

Rosa put a cool hand on Iridian's knee and was about to say something when Jessica opened the car door and tossed a plastic bag into the back seat. Iridian folded the scrap of paper and smashed it back into her fist, and with her free hand searched through the bag. She found cotton squares and hydrogen peroxide and Band-Aids that were too small for her cuts. There was no pen—no notebook, either.

She was going to tell Jessica to go back, but then she saw the pink tracks of tears that streaked down her sister's cheek, and the way she was white-knuckling the steering wheel.

"What happened?" Rosa asked.

"Nothing," Jessica replied.

As Jessica pulled out of the parking lot, tiny raindrops started to fall, but neither Jessica nor Rosa rolled their windows up. Iridian quietly tended to her wounds in the back seat, while Rosa extended her arm out the window to wiggle her fingers in the rain.

Even though her leg stung when the hydrogen peroxide hit the scrapes, it was a pain she could manage.

"Iridian," Rosa called back. "Have you ever touched someone's hand? Like, really studied it?"

Iridian had written so many descriptions: what it was like when a hand brushed against another hand, or stroked hair, or pinched tender skin. She'd had lines and lines, pages and pages. And now she could describe what it was like to care for broken skin—the soft pressure; the cool, gentle burn of the peroxide; the feeling of being very close but not all the way close.

But, no. She'd never touched someone's hand, not the way that Rosa meant, anyway.

"I hope you get the chance sometime," Rosa replied, watching raindrops bounce off her fingernails. "It's wonderful."

"Uh-huh," Iridian replied. It was all she could say. Maybe that was true—she was sure that hands could do wonderful things, but all Iridian could think about at the moment was hands doing destructive things: smashing against cheekbones, pulling hair, tearing book pages.

Iridian kept applying the peroxide until there was no more burn and her wounds stopped fizzing. Jessica kept driving, directionless, in circles it seemed. The winds were picking up. The receipt from the pharmacy flew from the back seat and out the window before Iridian could catch it.

"Where are we going?" Rosa eventually asked.

"Nowhere," Jessica replied. "Just around. Peter said he'd come by the house after his shift was over, and until then I'm just killing time." She paused. "He said he thinks Ana is trying to get us out of the house. That's why she's scaring us, ripping up Iridian's things, sending Rosa to search for the hyena."

"Leave the house and go where?" Rosa asked. "Where does Ana expect us to go?"

"Anywhere." Jessica let out a dry little laugh. "Or maybe she's lonely. Maybe she wants some company."

That wasn't funny. Iridian immediately thought of *The Witching Hour*, which doesn't have a happy ending. Whenever Iridian got close to the last few chapters, she always hoped that things would turn out differently. She didn't understand how a story could bring two characters together only to pull them so hopelessly apart. Why create something great only to destroy it? Even though the ending broke Iridian's heart every time, she never skipped it. She felt like the story was punishing her, but that it was a punishment well earned.

At the end of *The Witching Hour*, the ghost wins.

Jessica

HERE'S A SECRET: Something interesting happened four days after Ana died. Jessica was taking a shower. Just after turning on the water, she crouched down and peered into the drain. As the hot, hot water rolled down her back, Jessica pulled a clump of her older sister's hair from the trap. She knew it was Ana's because it was longer than hers was, and because a few of the strands were gray at the root. Jessica held the wet strands between her fingers for a few moments before putting the hair in her mouth and swallowing it.

Jessica

(early Monday, June 17th)

PETER SMELLED LIKE lemons, fake lemons like laundry detergent. Jessica could still smell it, even in her moldy old car, even over the dirt-smell of the rain. The lemon scent had been sucked up in her nostrils as she'd gasped and snorted against Peter's work shirt. She imagined it mixing with her cells and entering her bloodstream. She imagined it scraping against the walls of her organs and changing them, the way acid eats away at rock.

When Jessica had clung to Peter, she'd dug her nails into his lemon-scented shirt—*through* his lemon-scented shirt—and into his flesh. She'd created little hooks to hold him in place. She wondered if he still felt the impression of those hooks and if the small crescents made by her nails were still there in his skin. She wondered what she smelled like—she hoped it wasn't moldy like her car—and if her smell still hung in Peter's nose.

After almost an hour of doing loops through the neighborhood and the rain-soaked, near-empty streets of downtown San Antonio, Jessica stopped for gas at a corner store. She stood with her hand on the pump, leaning her hip against the back end of her car. There was an overhang that was supposed to protect her from the rain, but the spray was still hitting her sideways. The wind gusted and sent the raindrops swirling. Jessica was standing in a puddle. A wrapper from a red Starburst floated by her left shoe.

Rosa ran up, splashing across the parking lot. She'd gone into the store to get herself a bottle of water. She handed Iridian a small carton of chocolate milk through the window.

"Either save it for later or drink it all right now," Jessica told Iridian.

"What?"

"Save it, or drink it all right now and throw the carton away. I don't want you spilling and getting that smell in my car."

What she meant was that she didn't want the smell of milk to mix with or overpower the smell of lemons.

"What smell?" Iridian shot back. "I'm not a child. I know how to drink milk without spilling it."

Jessica waited as Iridian opened the carton and drank the milk all at once, in three large chugs. Then Iridian climbed out of the back seat to shove the empty carton into the overflowing garbage can between the pumps.

"There you go, princess," Iridian said, getting back into the car.

Jessica also got in, turned the ignition, and checked the time. Peter's shift ended at 6 a.m., in a little over thirty minutes. Peter hadn't told her what they would do once he got to her house. Maybe they would just sit on the floor and wait for Ana to tap on the window again. Or break something. Honestly, she'd settle for either. Or anything, really.

"We should go home now," Jessica said.

She expected at least one of her sisters to protest, but neither did.

Jessica pulled into the driveway, into the empty space where her dad usually parked his truck.

"Where do you think he went?" Iridian asked.

Jessica didn't answer. She realized she didn't really care anymore.

The sisters bolted out of the car and hustled through the rain to the door. Iridian was running so fast, she slid through the wet grass and lost her footing. Jessica and Rosa both reached out to catch her before she fell.

"Jess!"

Jessica spun around to see a rain-soaked John jogging up the sidewalk. Had he been lurking around this whole time?

"It's okay," Rosa whispered. "I can take care of it."

"I don't need you to take care of it," Jessica replied.

"I've been calling, sending messages," John said, crossing the yard. "Why haven't you answered?"

Jessica balked. John hadn't even acknowledged her sisters: one who he'd struck and the other who'd struck him. Instead, he was reducing everything that had happened that night to a little quarrel about Jessica not answering her fucking phone.

She thought back to the night she'd first kissed him, in front of everyone, in Evalin Uvalde's entryway. She'd wanted John to taste magical, cool like sweet tea, but he hadn't. She'd wanted him to tell her that she smelled like Ana—she'd doused herself in what was left of Ana's cotton-scented perfume before she'd left that night, screwing off the cap and slapping the liquid directly on her belly. She'd wanted John to tell her that she felt like Ana, that their skin was the same temperature or that they made the same sounds when naked.

He'd never said that. He'd also never told her what *she*, Jessica the individual, tasted like, felt like, sounded like. Instead, he always wanted to know, *When are you coming over?* and *Why aren't you answering your phone?*

Jessica wanted John to answer one question, and then she wanted nothing to do with him ever again.

"Did you see my sister die?" she asked.

John narrowed his gaze, pretending to be confused. Oh, she knew that look. It was one of Rafe's go-to expressions.

"Jessica," John said, "can we go inside, please?"

"Did you see her?" Jessica urged. "Did you *hear* her? She shouted. We heard her cry out."

John spread his arms wide, in a way that also reminded Jessica of her father. It was this big lost-for-words T-shape. It meant, *What do you want me to say?*

Jessica handed Rosa her keys. "Can you two wait in the car?"

"In the *car*?" Iridian balked.

"I'm going to take John inside to dry off," Jessica said. "I'll just be a minute. I promise."

Rosa's eyebrow hiked up.

"Bathroom's off the kitchen," Jessica said as she opened the door for John. "To the right. There are towels there."

John trudged through the dark house, and Jessica was left alone. The living room was a disaster. Pages from the notebook she'd given Iridian were strewn about, on the carpet and on the couch. The television screen was smashed to crystals, as if someone had pitched a bowling ball into the center of it.

"You're mad," Jessica whispered. "I get it."

She took a step forward, and paper crunched lightly under her foot.

"But I don't think you're mad at us."

Jessica waited for a sign that she'd been heard. Iridian had mentioned smelling oranges, but all Jessica could smell was the dust and mildew that always clung to the walls and old carpet.

"I brought someone for you," Jessica said, just as John came out of the back bathroom, rubbing his head with a towel.

Jessica made sure she was between John and the front door. From where she was standing, she could see through the living room and back into the kitchen. She could hear the fridge buzzing, and an ice cube drop from the door to the floor.

"I know you saw her," Jessica said. "You had to have. You watched Ana die, and then you drove away."

There was a shadow—a blur—that appeared at the right edge of the door to the kitchen. It was a figure, a dark, girl-shaped figure in a dark doorway, about Jessica's height.

Jessica had to force her eyes back to John, had to force her feet to stay rooted and her hands from flying up to her racing heart.

"I was scared," John said. He hung his head and shook it. "I didn't know what to do."

The figure behind John glided fully into the doorway

and stopped. It wasn't as clear as a person, but it was more than a hand on a curtain.

"You were scared?" Jessica asked. She started to tremble as laughter built up inside her.

Peter had told her she needed to fight for herself. She didn't need to do that, though, because she had her sisters.

"I don't want to lose you." John reached for Jessica's hand.

She let him take it, but only for a moment. "It's not that you don't want to lose *me*," she said, pulling away and stepping back. "It's that you're scared of being alone. Wait here," she added. "I just need to get something out of my car."

As Jessica turned to the door, John, for the first time, looked around and took in the destruction around him— the paper and broken glass. He started to say something, but by then Jessica was already outside, pulling the door closed. She had her key out, ready to thrust and twist into the lock. She was ready to seal John into the house. It was a terrible thing to do—lock a person in with a ghost—but Jessica was a terrible person.

But then the bolt clicked on its own. Jessica knew she'd always remember that smooth sound: the heavy thunk, heavy like a long, satisfying exhale.

John hit the door and called out, but Jessica backed away from the house, taking ankle-deep steps into the mucky yard. The storm was now in full force. Rain struck her from every direction, and the sky was booming, lit up gray and bright white by the lightning. She heard Rosa and Iridian running toward her from the car.

"She was there," Jessica gasped. "I saw her."

John called out again. The pitch of his voice was higher now. It was like when she was hiding in the church, and he was growing frantic when he couldn't find her. She'd done nothing then, and she'd do nothing now. Jessica closed her eyes and tipped her face up to the rain.

Rosa came up to her side and linked their arms together. "You did the right thing," she said.

John pounded on the door again, over and over. Suddenly, he stopped. Then the screaming started. Only someone standing close to the house could hear it, though. The roar of the storm was so loud.

Iridian

(early Monday, June 17th)

JESSICA'S EYES WERE closed. She looked peaceful, like she was listening to music, like the storm was her favorite song.

Linked together with Jessica, Rosa's eyes were closed, too. Their lids were sealed tight. Rosa dropped her sister's keys into the grass. Jessica might have been soaking in the sound of John's fear, but Rosa was fine-tuned to something else farther away.

Finally, Rosa exhaled, long and slow, like she was deflating. Then her eyes popped open.

"I'm sorry," she said. "I have to go."

Rosa unlaced herself from her sister and took off across the yard. Within moments, she'd vanished between two houses. Without Rosa, Jessica seemed to sway, like she'd lost her anchor. She stared at the front door, then in the direction in which Rosa had run, then back to the door.

"We should find her." Iridian picked up Jessica's keys from where Rosa had dropped them. "Jess!"

Iridian yanked her sister's wrist, but Jessica jerked away, causing Iridian to tip back. She tried to dig her heels into the ground but slipped and fell palms-first into the mud.

"What's your problem?" Iridian barked, wiping the splatter from her eyes.

"She'll be fine!" Jessica replied. "She goes out by herself all the time."

"Not during a *thunderstorm*!"

Lightning silently split the sky, and for a moment longer, Jessica stood facing the house. John's screams had died out, and Iridian imagined him, curled up in a ball just inside the front door, with his head in his hands, weeping. When she had a pen and paper again, she'd fill up line after line describing him there—his body position cramped, his breathless paralysis caused by fear.

"You're right," Jessica said. "Let's go."

Jessica took her keys and then grabbed Iridian by the waist and hoisted her up to standing. Together, they marched to Jessica's car, but at a clap of thunder so close and loud, Iridian startled and again lost her footing. She threw her hand out to check her balance and realized it was empty. The piece from her notebook—the one that she'd been holding in her fist—was gone. Frantic, she fell to her knees and started to claw at the wet grass.

Jessica tried again to pull her up. "Are we going or not?"

"Stop!" Iridian yelled. "Just give me a second."

Iridian's limbs were slick with rain and mud, but still Jessica managed to wrestle her up off the ground and drag her the few feet to her car.

"Wait!" Iridian cried out.

Thrust into the back seat, and without her scrap of paper, Iridian folded forward in half and covered her head with her hands.

Iridian had no heart for John. She didn't care about the low moans and high whines she heard before Jessica closed the door to the house, sounds that mimicked the wind. She cared about that paper more than she cared about almost anything. In that moment, she cared about that paper more than she cared about her sisters, including Ana. As they drove through the neighborhood, Iridian half-heartedly looked for Rosa while mourning the loss of her piece of paper. Occasionally, Jessica would call back to her and ask if she could see anything, and Iridian would just shake her head and mumble.

Eventually, Iridian peeked at her empty hand and saw blotches of blue ink. *I'm sorry* had transferred to her skin. The words were blurry and backward, but they were there.

"Jess. My paper."

"I'm not going to—"

"Please just turn around," Iridian croaked. "My paper. I dropped it. We can find it, and then we'll find Rosa."

"Iridian!" Jessica shouted. "Shut up! This was your idea. This isn't about your fucking piece of paper right now."

Iridian bolted upright and reached forward across the console to grab the steering wheel. She pulled it clockwise, in the direction of the curb, but instead of stopping, the car went into a skid. Jessica shoved Iridian away and was able to pump the brakes and prevent the car from going into a spin. They were stopped, at a diagonal, in the middle of an empty intersection. Iridian was wheezing and could feel the hard thuds of her heart.

"*What the fuck?*" Jessica shouted. "Don't fucking do that again!"

"I'm sorry," Iridian said. "I'm sorry. I wasn't thinking."

Iridian wanted to fold back into herself, crawl into the fabric of the seat. She met Jessica's eyes in the rearview mirror.

"It's okay," Jessica said, easing the car through the intersection. "Just . . . I'll get you another notebook. Let's find Rosa first, alright?"

Rosa

AT THE HEART level, all animals are different. Birds have small hearts that beat very fast. Once, at a petting zoo, Rosa held a chick up to her ear, and the sound it made wasn't like a *thump, thump, thump* but more like a *whoosh, whoosh, whoosh*, like water tumbling around and around in the washing machine. The birds that flew around Southtown during the summer had hearts like tiny engines. They were always moving. They propelled themselves from tree branch to tree branch and telephone line to telephone line. Rosa imagined their heartbeats were so fast that, if she could hear them, they would sound like drumrolls. If their hearts beat that fast, then maybe, sometimes, they conked out mid-flight, and then dropped straight to the ground.

Squirrels also have small hearts that beat fast, though obviously not as fast as birds'. Rosa had never held a squirrel up to her ear, but she'd watched them. Like birds, they propel themselves off tree branches and telephone lines. Sometimes they freeze mid-step because they hear something in the distance or notice something out of the corner of their eye. Their arms and legs and head stay motionless, but their hearts still pound against their ribs. Also, their tails never stop swishing. It's like they can't help it.

Fireflies have tiny hearts that create electricity. Crickets have tiny hearts that fuel tiny legs that scrape together to create a song that will bring them a mate.

The crickets at night are not just chirping, and the birds in the morning are not just chattering. The sounds they make come from their hearts.

When Rosa first started sitting in the backyard on Sunday mornings and her sisters asked what she was doing, she told them she was trying to talk to the animals. She wished she hadn't ever said that. It sounded kind of ridiculous. She didn't want to *talk* to the animals. That was impossible. It also made no sense. Maybe *communicate* was a better word? She just wanted to be able to hear things, and she wanted the creatures of this world to know they were being heard. That's all. When a squirrel sat up on the telephone wires, flicking its tail, Rosa didn't know what it was thinking, and she didn't need to know what it was thinking. If anything, she wanted him—the squirrel—to know that *she* was thinking of *him*.

The Torres family had never had a dog, and, until Rafe hit that one a week ago, Rosa had never been able to lay her head against a dog's silky fur and listen to its heartbeat. At first that dog's heart was beating fast, but then it started to rumble. Then it lurched and twisted. The dog was bleeding pretty bad, and whining softly, and if Rosa could've done something to make it hurt less in its final moments she would have. Finally, its heart beat once more—*hard*—and shuddered. The dog exhaled and then was silent. Rosa counted out a full fifteen seconds, and the dog didn't move. That's when she knew it was dead. She wished she'd done the same thing with Ana, a year ago in the front yard, but she'd been too scared. Before the ambulance came, she should've put her ear to Ana's back, up between her shoulder blades, and counted to fifteen. She should've listened to her heart and said *please*, as if a heart could hear her request. But she didn't.

People were animals, too, and when they got sick or scared, their hearts gave out.

Rosa

(early Monday, June 17th)

THERE WAS NO doubt the hyena was close—in the neighborhood somewhere, maybe in one of the alleys. Rosa had heard it laughing. When she was standing in her yard with her sisters and all the lights in the house had gone out, she'd heard the animal's wild laugh, clear as day.

So Rosa ran into the dim space between two houses. She stopped in a patch of waterlogged grass. Thunder cracked. The sky flashed bright white, and then the sound rose up again, like a bobbing chuckle.

With the humidity in the air, Rosa felt like she weighed an extra twenty pounds. The heavy, electric air tugged at the tiny hairs on her arms.

Storms, she knew, brought out certain instincts in animals. The birds, normally quiet at this time of night, were getting nervous. They squawked and flew around in crazy loops. They heard thunder, and they saw those flashes of lightning, and they got scared. They wanted shelter in a warm and comfortable place.

Jessica used to do the same thing. If a thunderstorm broke out in the middle of the night, she'd run down to Ana's room to seek shelter. Jessica thought no one else in the family knew about that, but of course Rosa did.

The dogs were barking so loud and from so many different places. They were driven mad by the thunder. Rosa could still hear the hyena and its laugh, but she couldn't tell where it was coming from. She'd turn down an alley, thinking she was on the right track, and then the sound would come from right behind her. She'd spin around, and the laugh would suddenly seem far away. Rosa cried out in frustration. There was another clap of thunder, and after that, Rosa thought she heard another laugh, but not the hyena's laugh. It was, undeniably, Ana's laugh.

It was different from the high, cruel laugh she and her sisters had heard back at the house on the day of the block party. That one was meant to frighten, Rosa thought, but this one was genuine and joyful. Ana would laugh like this when the four of them were little and would be playing in the yard together in the summer, barefoot in the grass, racing one another from the edge of the back porch to the fence, chasing one another with the hose or having cartwheel contests.

Rosa heard Ana's laugh again, coming from the street. She swerved and ran back toward it. She could help. She *would* help. It's what she was made to do.

Human hearts are very complicated. They can pull a person this way, then that. They can convince someone easy things are hard, or cloudy things are clear.

Jessica
(early Monday, June 17th)

JESSICA'S WIPER BLADE flicked across her windshield. Nothing was there. The blade flicked again across her windshield, and there the animal was, standing perfectly still in the road. A gray hyena against a gray sky and gray street. Her headlights caught the reflection of two eyes. They weren't startled or scared, but intense, as if they were urging her onward. It was only when Iridian gripped the seat in front of her and shouted that Jessica braked hard and braced for the impact. The sound of the animal colliding with the car was quieter than Jessica would've expected, and it came in two parts. First, there was a wet thud against the front bumper, and then another, more violent thud as the meat of the body was pulled under the tires.

The car went on a few more feet before skidding to a stop. Jessica bucked forward in her seat and clung to the steering wheel for balance. Squinting through the windshield, she saw the wipers still swishing, uselessly tossing sheets of rainwater side to side. Her headlights were feebly illuminating the empty street.

"Shit," Jessica breathed. She looked into the rearview mirror and saw the hyena's dark, unmoving form. "What the fuck just happened?"

"It was a dog, I think," Iridian said.

A howl, animal-like but not quite, cut through the night and rose over the thumps of rain. Initially, Jessica thought the piercing sound came from the hyena, and she half expected to see it rise, all herky-jerky, and stumble out of the road. But when the howl rose up again, louder and more mournful, Jessica realized the sound came from a person, a girl, her sister. In the rearview mirror, Jessica watched Rosa run out from between a couple of houses and into the middle of the street. She was lit up an oozy blood red by the taillights and the rain, and then dropped to her knees in front of the hyena. She swept the long rope of her hair over one ear and leaned down over the animal.

In the back seat, Iridian sucked in a hard breath. She

was staring in horror through the rain-streaked windshield at the murky yellow headlights of an advancing pickup truck. That truck was headed straight toward Rosa and the hyena, both of which had merged into one dark mass on a dark road.

"No!" Jessica frantically slammed down on her horn, but the truck didn't halt and Rosa didn't leave her animal. "No, no, *no!*"

Jessica threw open her door and ran out into the road. She heard Iridian shout something, a warning maybe, but she didn't look back. Jessica knew, just as every other person in Southtown knew, that Rosa was the good sister, the one worth saving. Jessica was the expendable sister, the one with the heart too hot, the one who locked boys into houses with ghosts, the one with nothing to give but anger.

She could feel that hot heart, burning rather than beating, as she plowed through the warm rain toward her little sister.

"Rosa! *Rosa!*"

Jessica lost traction. As she fell, her palm slammed into the gritty asphalt, but she managed to push herself up and plow forward. She shouted her sister's name again, and finally Rosa looked up, startled, as Jessica hauled her off the ground and flung her toward the curb. Jessica slipped again—this time falling hard onto both her hands and knees. She heard, too close, the squeal of tires against a wet road. She felt heat, like the hottest wind, push against her and pin her down.

The impact was quieter than she would've expected. There was a dull thud as the front end of the truck collided with her ribs, and then another as she was pulled under one of the tires. It hurt, but she'd felt worse.

Jessica could breathe, but she couldn't swallow. She knew she was on the ground, facedown, and that her head was turned to the side because pebbles from the road were smashed against her cheek and chin, and rainwater trickled into her open mouth. She may have been trying to talk—saying what, she didn't know. There was something wrong with her ears. She couldn't hear the rain or the car anymore, but she could hear what was going on *inside* her body. Her lungs were gurgling. There were lots of little pops. Her blood, its swishing, was so loud, making such a racket. She heard someone's voice. It took a second, but she realized that voice belonged to Peter. The sound of Peter's voice—even though he seemed so panicked about something—didn't make her angry. She saw his shoes, the off-white sneakers he always wore to work, and she tried to move her mouth, puckering her lips like she was trying to give those shoes a kiss. The air smelled sort of like oranges. She saw the muddy toes of rubber boots and a flash of red fabric. It was Rosa. Jessica's whole spine shivered. Rosa was safe. Her sister had been saved. Jessica tried to cry out with happiness and relief, but she couldn't get the sound to rise from her throat. Rosa knelt down in front of Jessica and then leaned forward. The rainwater continued to trickle into Jessica's mouth. Her lungs kept popping. She heard Rosa breathing, and she felt the lightest pressure, at the center of her chest, right there above her heart.

Iridian

(Sunday, July 7th)

IT WAS SUNDAY, so Iridian slept in, then went downstairs to the kitchen to sit on the counter, eat chocolate puffs, and watch Rosa in the backyard. She was still up on the counter when a car blared its horn out front.

"Rosa!" Jessica yelled from the couch in the living room, where she was watching cartoons on a new television. "The Matas are here!"

Outside, Rosa bolted from her chair. She ran into and through the house, calling out her goodbyes.

After finishing her cereal, Iridian went upstairs to her room and started reading *The Witching Hour*. In her days since the accident, Rosa had helped her sister sort through all the pages and put the book back together—mostly back together. Some pages were still missing, as was the back cover, but it was good enough. Iridian read for a couple of hours, and then she started writing. There might be a time when she would write in her notebooks again, but for now, she wrote on the walls. She started with her old stories. She was surprised by how much she remembered. Things were still in pieces—paragraphs were unfinished; sentences were unfinished—but things had always been in pieces when it came to her stories. That was fine. At least words were being put down. She could see them, and, if they wanted, her sisters could see them, too.

At first, Iridian wrote standing, at eye level, in as straight a line as she could for as long as she could. Eventually, she would come up against an obstacle— a piece of furniture or a window—and she would write around it. After a while, she was forced to sit and write on baseboards and on the molding that went around the doors. She wrote on the back wall of her closet and on the inside of her bathroom cabinet doors. At a certain point, her stories leaked out into the hallway, toward Jessica's room, then on the staircase railing, and on the stairs themselves. There was peacock blue everywhere.

It would take some time, but eventually there wouldn't be a surface without words on it. That was the goal. She knew in time the ink would fade, and in even more time, the walls of the house would split and crumble, but as she scrawled down her scraps of stories, her descriptions of hair and voices and the smells of skin, her growing list of possible character names, she felt like she was constructing a monument, something that would be there forever. Iridian didn't know if she was happy, but at least she felt like she was doing something significant. Doing something significant made her feel significant.

Iridian had been sitting in the hall upstairs, writing on the bathroom door, when she heard Peter let himself in. There were no rules about boys in the house anymore because there was no Rafe anymore. After Ana had smashed the television, Rafe had fled to Norma's, spent the night, and then, before sunrise, made off with a shoebox containing four thousand dollars. Jessica had maybe seen him late one night when she was in the hospital, recovering from a punctured lung and broken femur. She thought he'd been standing by her bedside, weeping loudly into his hands, but that could've been a drug-hazed delusion. Regardless, the girls hadn't seen their father in three weeks, but a few days ago a brand-new television had been delivered to the house, so they knew their father was out there somewhere, feeling guilty and spending Norma Galván's money.

Peter had canceled his trip to Mexico. He and Jessica were trying to whisper to each other, but Iridian could still hear what they were saying. She wrote as fast as she could, trying to copy their conversation word for word.

"You're late," Jessica said.

"Traffic was bad," Peter replied. "I didn't know what kind you wanted, so I got you chocolate."

Jessica slurped a straw and then said, "Vanilla next time."

"Wow," Peter said. "Ungrateful."

"I know. I suck. Someone should run me over with his truck."

Jessica laughed at herself, then immediately winced from the strain.

Iridian kept writing, but she could see, out of the corner of her eye, light starting to flicker from the lamp in her bedroom. The light was from the same lamp Rosa had ripped from the wall downstairs and swung at the men who hurt Iridian and her sisters. They'd brought it up to their room. It was theirs now. The light blinked out, then came back on. It did that sometimes.

Rosa

(Sunday, July 7th)

ROSA WAS IN church, and her attention had started to falter. Father Mendoza tended to repeat certain things in sermons and drive home the same points over and over. They were good points—about the virtues of being humble and forgiving—but still.

Rosa was thinking about how, on the way to church, the Matas' car had passed Peter Rojas's truck. He was coming to check in on Jessica again, which was nice. Peter was nice, but he hadn't been right about Ana. Rosa had never believed Ana's purpose in coming back was to get her and her sisters out of their house. That would've meant they would've had to split up, or split up even more than they already had in the year since Ana died. Rosa knew that Ana had come back to convince her and her sisters to stay together. They needed one another. Rosa knew this for a *fact*, and she'd known it since she'd placed her ear against her sister's chest and heard her heart stop beating. Jessica had shuddered. Several seconds had passed. Rosa had whispered *please*, and Jessica's heart had started to beat again. Rosa had made a heart beat. Before that, she'd only made a heart stop.

There was movement on the pew. Walter was there, next to her. His hand was spread out, palm-down on the wood. Rosa's hand was also there, also spread out. Walter's pinkie finger wiggled a little, then shifted toward hers until it brushed up against the side of Rosa's hand. Rosa didn't smile, but her whole body felt warmer. There was so much magic in small things.

After church, when Walter's mom had dropped her off back at her house, Rosa nearly stepped on a piece of paper in the front yard, wedged between two blades of grass. The paper was lined, but the lines were pale, bleached from the sun and rain. Most of the blue ink was completely faded. As she crouched down to pick it up, she saw that there were only two legible words: *I want*

It could've meant anything.

Acknowledgments

Thanks to my teachers, my students, my colleagues, my family (Guy!), and my friends. This novel was a tricky one, loosely bound for a long time by the idea of combining three sisters, the confining setting of their house/neighborhood, and a ghost. A huge amount of thanks goes to my agent, Claire Anderson-Wheeler at Regal Hoffmann, for seeing a story worth pursuing and being patient with me as I figured it all out. Of course, thanks to Krestyna Lypen and Elise Howard at Algonquin Young Readers (and everyone at AYR), for *also* seeing a story worth pursuing, and for their wisdom and enthusiasm. Courtney Summers and Stephanie Kuehn read early versions of this novel and offered kind words, and for that, I am grateful. A major source of inspiration for this story was *How the García Girls Lost Their Accents* by Julia Alvarez, and, as such, I am stunned and honored to have her give praise to my Torres sisters.

Other sources of inspiration: The chorus of the boys across the street at Hector's house is a nod to *The Virgin Suicides* by Jeffrey Eugenides. Iridian's favorite book, *The Witching Hour* by Anne Rice, is a book I wish I'd written and have read over and over again. The ultimate source of inspiration for this novel, though that may not seem so obvious now, is Shakespeare's *King Lear*. In the play, the phrase "tigers, not daughters" is hurled out as a harsh insult against Regan and Goneril, but I've always loved this line, and wanted to write a story about daughters and their father in which those words perhaps meant something completely different, and weren't an insult at all.

Lastly, thanks to all who have read or boosted my stories. I appreciate you more than you'll ever know.